MW00830594

BELLA FAYRE

SISTERS of the SCORNED

A DONNA DESHAYNE NOVEL

Blessings !
Bella
Fayre '20

Copyright © 2017 by Bella Fayre
Bellafayre@ucanpublishing.com
All rights reserved.
Printed and Bound in the United States of America

Published and Distributed by:
UCAN Publishing, LLC
P.O. Box 51616
Myrtle Beach, S.C. 29579
www.ucanpublishing.com

Editing:
EV Proofreading
www.evproofreading.com

Interior Layout and Cover Design:
TWA Solutions
www.twasolutions.com

ISBN: 978-0-9909310-6-5
Library of Congress Control Number: 2017953025

First Print: January 2018

This is a work of fiction. Names, characters, businesses, groups, organizations, places, events, and incidents are the product of the author's imagination and/or used in a fictitious manner. Any resemblance to actual places, persons, living or dead, actual groups or actual events is purely coincidental.

No part of this book may be reproduced, stored in a retrieval system or transmitted in any form or by any means without the prior written permission of the publisher, except by a reviewer who may quote brief passages in a review to be printed in a newspaper, magazine, or journal.

For inquires, contact the publisher.

PRAISE FOR

SISTERS OF THE SCORNED

"Bella Fayre offers us another powerful Donna DeShayne mystery of substance and history wrapped in an engaging, sophisticated novel. Her characters and descriptions give us a glimpse of a tumultuous time when the world seemed off its axis. If we do not study history, we are certainly doomed to repeat it."   Ann Jeffries, Author, the *Family Reunion —Wisdom of the Ancestors* series.

"*Sisters of the Scorned* is a must read for everyone! A remarkable story told by one of the best, Bella Fayre. You'll feel the terror of Hitler's reign, the despair of the citizens, and cheer the bravery of those who survived. Well done!"   J.A. Meinecke, Author, *A Woman to Reckon With*

"Bella Fayre has captured the essence of a tragic time in our history and then used actual details to weave a realistic tale of fiction. A group of female survivors from World War II concentration camps use their strength of purpose to carve out a new life. Intrigue, combined with intellect, are used in a winding path through time and history to an ending you'll never expect. Once you pick up this book, you won't be able to put it down until the surprising conclusion."   Rebecca Bridges, Author, *After the Reunion*

"*Sisters of the Scorned* is another winner for Bella Fayre. This historical fiction doesn't disappoint with a storyline full of twists and turns, which keeps the reader fully engaged. Don't miss this one." Nancy Engle, Author, *Murder at Mount Joy* and *Image of Perfection*

"As Fayre skillfully weaved together the threads of two generations, I found myself completely submerged into the mystery of who, what, where, when, and why. Engrossing!" Carole O'Neill, Author, *Hidden Truth*

Other Writings by Bella Fayre

❧

Maelstroms of the Silent

Guardian of the Damned

"When the people fear their government,

there is tyranny;

when the government fears the people,

there is liberty."

Thomas Jefferson

In Memory Of

Eliezer (Elie) Wiesel
September 30, 1928 - July 2, 2016

Survivor of Auschwitz and Buchenwald concentration camps

Author, professor, activist

Chairman of the United States Holocaust Museum – 1980-1986

Nobel Peace Prize Recipient - 1986

Presidential Medal of Freedom

Congressional Gold Medal

Grand Officer of the Order of the Star of Romania

Grand Cross of the National Order of the Legion of Honour

Honorary Knighthood

Notable Works: *Night* - 1960

"We must take sides. Neutrality helps the Oppressor, never the Victim.

Silence encourages the Tormentor, never the Tormented.

Sometimes we must interfere. When human lives are endangered, when human indignity is in jeopardy, national borders and sensitivities become

Irrelevant...

And action is the only remedy to Indifference, the most

Insidious danger of all."

Elie Wiesel, Nobel Peace Prize Acceptance Speech, 1986

CHAPTER ONE

"Times does not heal all wounds; there are those
that remain painfully open."

Elie Wiesel

She was an old woman now. The mirror told no lies. Nearly eighty-six years of age, the march of depleting cells in her body signaled a reminder of now-numbered days. Never fully recovered from the events of her tumultuous past, periods of undefined fatigue and exhaustion grew more frequent as she aged. Now, in the final months, she would often lie curled up on her bed guarding her meager reserves.

Nowadays, in her wakeful hours, whether day or night, distant memories presented themselves. Resolute in their entry, they insisted on acknowledgement. She resisted the intrusion at first. After all, she had put them to rest years ago, or so she thought, but alas, they were insinuating themselves toward further recognition, seeking clarity and conveyance, even now at this late stage in her life. So be it. It was the very least she could do. She was willing to salute the past, allowing credence, despite painful recall.

There was no question she was luckier than most; that she knew. Finally finding love, she spent her remaining years cloistered in a cocoon of devotion and fulfillment, producing a family from which she would realize a different strength and will; at last, a final semblance of normalcy.

Her husband, Jacob Schmidt, presented years later a new beginning, a fresh start, a chance to put the past behind. How she had luxuriated in his benign underpinnings of emotional comfort and presence. She remembered such as a child, but it was lost so suddenly, cast to the throes of demonic and despotic forces.

Jacob was a beautiful, tender man of deep personal faith and devotion to family and friends. It would be through his love she would realize the full measure of her womanhood. She often marveled at the redeeming qualities of love when applied to once-wounded and wretched souls like herself. Bearing personal witness, her eventual awakening as a child of God was due to the soothing balm provided by the love of her husband. Oh, how she had come to adore, and even worship her life partner, and yet he had no clue of the woman she became after her experiences and before they met. It would be a secret she would guard to her dying day.

Now, in the final stages of life, and in the loving care of her two adult children, she lacked for nothing. Her children remained her strength after Jacob's death ten years earlier. It was a beautiful passing during which she was able to declare her undying love and devotion to the man who saved her from drowning in a pool of deprecated memories related to childhood despair before he entered her life.

Her children knew nothing of her past. There was no need to reveal the horror and the shame, or the eventual resolve of the sisters. Jacob's entrance into her life presented a new beginning and a fresh start. There was no need to revisit the past. Until now.

The memories swept into her thoughts with untold speed at times, shaking her psyche. In these unexpected and uninvited moments, she would pray for full reclamation, underscoring her instinct that her final passing was near.

Perhaps it was still possible to reconcile the past with the present. While some would suggest that time heals all things, in this she still had strength to argue. In her final moments, spent in lifetime review, she would conclude…time can only abate the pain of recall.

Nonetheless, it was the season to remember long-forgotten days, to bestow a blessing on the end resolve. It was time to herald memories, to acknowledge them in the bosom of necessary dispatch, even those which still blistered the heart. After all, she concluded—in the end of days, and in the final analysis—all we have are memories.

Just days before, she feebly gathered the tangible reminders of her past, fingering each item as she looked at them through a lens of painful remembrance before placing them in packages she would seal and make ready for delivery. It would be her attempt to address unfinished business.

She hoped, as she noted the now-labored beating of her heart, the content of the parcels would be received in a manner meriting further examination. Perhaps not. Long ago, she learned to guard against disappointment related to expectation.

In any event, the outcome was now out of her hands. Her final effort would be her tribute to the once-wretched sisters who came together and devised a plan. She had come to respect each and every one of them in their resolve not to be silent, but to instead reconcile the evil. After a thorough and satisfying review, she took her last breath before eternal rest, to be forever enjoined with her beloved Jacob.

CHAPTER TWO

"Hey girlfriend! I'm calling to remind you of the twins' birthday party this coming Saturday. Can you believe it has been ten years? Call me back."

It was Sunday morning. Donna DeShayne usually slept late on Sundays. Her lifelong friend and neighbor, Carole Tandermann was up bright and early as usual. Carole was a morning person, especially after her third cup of coffee.

They were steadfast friends since childhood, though Carole was twelve years older than Donna. Carole's parents were of Jewish descent and lived, for a time, in the borough of Manhattan, New York, before moving to East Brunswick, New Jersey, when Carole was nearly six years old. Carole's father established a pharmacy in East Brunswick, and her mother, an attorney, practiced bankruptcy law in Manhattan. Carole eventually earned a degree in psychiatry and in time married Gavin, also Jewish, who was older than she by nearly fifteen years. They remained deeply in love.

Donna's mother, Doris Lewis, divorced her husband after twelve years of marriage and moved from Philadelphia, with her young child, to East Brunswick, New Jersey. Doris raised her daughter as a single mother, through grit and glory, whichever came first. Though she never remarried, Doris Lewis held two jobs during the week, and often another on the weekend, setting an example for Donna who, in adulthood, evidenced her mother's strongly-focused drive. Such an example would serve Donna well.

Eventually, with Carole's encouragement, Donna obtained a degree in psychiatry, with a specialty in forensics. She then moved to the South Carolina coast to join her best friend in a psychiatric practice established by Carole twelve years earlier. Later, after her husband's heart attack, Carole turned her clients over to Donna and retired from medicine. Carole quickly grew bored with retirement, and being a coffee connoisseur, opened a small coffee shop in River Town, South Carolina. Within seven years, one shop turned into six cafés along the Grand Strand, a name given to the sixty miles of South Carolina coastline. Bolstered by an online site for coffee sales, business was booming and Carole was in her glory. Coffee was her ultimate drug of choice and she knew every bean from every country. Her Beans cafés, favored by locals and tourists alike, were immensely popular.

Carole and Gavin Tandermann were devoted, not only to each other, but also to their friends. A retired FBI agent, Gavin excelled at baking and cooking, hosting dinner parties at the drop of a hat. Carole often bragged to Donna of their sex life, details of which she felt she could do without. Nonetheless, she admired the obvious devotion her friends shared for nearly thirty years.

Donna's longing for her own soul mate and life partner became a reality after she met Ken Daniels, a detective on the Horry County Police Force, who became the stabilizing force in Donna's life after her disastrous marriage to her first husband, Donald Calavacchi. A convicted felon, Calavacchi died after escaping from prison and a failed attempt on Donna's life.

Donna's twenty-year psychiatric career was punctuated by intermittent, but highly successful undertakings in forensic crime investigation. Now well known as a consultant in challenging cases, she was sought after by law enforcement agencies across the country for assistance in solving the, heretofore, unsolvable cases. Nearly five years ago, she began doing consulting work exclusively after turning her psychiatric practice over to another competent professional.

Having just returned the night before from a successful resolution of an investigation in Atlanta, Donna was glad to be home. When she got out of bed mid-morning, the aroma of coffee beckoned her to the kitchen. Pouring a cup for herself, she was grateful to Ken for preparing it especially for her. She stood at the window, coffee cup in hand, gazing at him atop the riding lawn mower. The morning was humid and warm. His muscular arms already glistened with sweat. She smiled as she watched him work. He was always a delight to observe, with a physique revealing his focused workouts at the gym. How she loved this man. After twenty years together, he could still make her dizzy with desire.

He must have sensed her presence because he turned toward the window and blew a kiss to her. She returned the gesture, not forgetting the real kisses the night before in their lovemaking. Ken was an exceptional lover, never failing to bring her to heightened states of ecstasy each and every time. She sighed in satisfaction before turning away from the window to return Carole's call.

"Your prodigal friend has returned," she announced when Carole answered.

"It's about time! Are you satisfied with your investigation?" Carole asked, mindful Donna was often away.

"It's a closed case and the outcome was successful. I'm home again. That's all that matters. Are the twins ten years old already?"

"That they are, and their birthday party is on Saturday at our place at four o'clock. Mary said she wouldn't miss it for the world."

"How is Mary doing?"

"Grand! She is near to completing her second year in grad school and focused on her master's in psychology. Gavin and I couldn't be more proud of our granddaughter."

"It is she who should be proud of you and Gavin," Donna said, remembering the years of effort. "After all, without you two, there may not have been any number of welcoming events."

Donna remembered the supportive efforts Gavin and Carole Tandermann extended years earlier toward Mary's parents, Saul and Lacy Sue Larson. Lacy Sue was a patient of Donna's at the time, recovering from a severely abusive relationship with her first husband prior to his death. It was the Tandermanns who took Lacy Sue, and her second husband, Saul, under their wings, giving them the support and emotional guidance they so desperately needed, while Donna provided the mental-health support. It paid off handsomely. Presently, Saul had a successful lawn care business, while Lacy Sue was the administrator of a local assisted-living center. The couple, now raising three children, Mary and a set of twins, a son they named Gavin, and a daughter they named Carole, born nearly ten years after Mary, were a thriving family.

"So you're coming?" Carole asked.

"Why wouldn't we? After all, Mary and the twins are family, girlfriend."

There was a prolonged pause. "Are you there?" Donna asked her friend,

"I'm here, but a bit distracted. Gavin received a parcel yesterday. He's been quiet ever since. I've never seen him like this."

"What kind of parcel?"

"You know. A package. A simple one."

"That doesn't tell me much. What was in it?"

"I don't think it's my place to tell. I'd rather it come from Gavin."

"You're being highly mysterious," Donna countered. There was a deep sigh on the other end.

"It's only because I don't know what is in the package. Gavin looked at its contents and went into his office for hours. He's been in a funk ever since, and very protective of the package. When I asked what was in it, he didn't respond. That's not like him."

Donna picked up on the frightened tone in her friend's voice. "Tell me what you're really concerned about." Donna knew her friend well, not forgetting she was also a retired psychiatrist.

Carole didn't respond immediately. Donna waited until her friend was ready. "I know Gavin like the back of my hand. My Gavin is caring, supportive, and trustworthy, my lover and best friend. The Gavin I have seen in the last twenty-four hours, I don't know. That Gavin is distant and remote. He even refused sex last night!"

"Heaven forbid," Donna responded with a touch of sarcasm. "Did you ever stop to consider its okay to take a break from sex and it doesn't mean your relationship is going down the tubes?"

"You don't understand," Carole suggested. "I thought if I were more demonstrative than usual, it would make him feel better, and maybe he would share with me. He didn't. Donna, he's never shut me out before."

Donna nodded and smiled to herself, before responding gently. "Back up, girlfriend. Your experience as a psychiatrist should remind you Gavin may be doing nothing more than processing and will share when he's ready."

Carole sighed deeply. "I sound whiny, don't I? The thing is, when it comes to Gavin, I'm not able to apply professional parameters. I never have. It's a weakness of mine."

"A lovely one, at that. Let Gavin share when he's ready. The Gavin I know has always been very open and honest. I don't expect that to change."

After ending the call, Donna settled in for the week. It felt good to be home, with no pending needs for her expertise. She caught up on long overdue projects, mostly those involving repotting several overgrown houseplants, and some spring cleaning efforts.

The birthday party for the Larson twins went off without a hitch. Everyone had a grand time, adults included. Donna and Ken spent the afternoon helping with kid sports and events. Gavin and Carole oversaw the grilling of hot dogs and hamburgers, and their big sister, Mary, brought in the magician. Lacy Sue and Saul, the parents, took charge of the decorations and presents. Nearly fifteen children and seven adults had the time of their lives.

Gavin, ever the photographer, was busy taking pictures throughout the afternoon. Donna observed him, mindful of Carole's concern. While he appeared engaged and available, there were glancing moments when a look came across his face and he quieted. Adjusting himself, he continued on as the proud grandfather of three, serving food, assisting in the sports, and cutting two cakes he personally designed with super heroes, one super hero boy for young Gavin, and one super hero girl for young Carole.

The day quieted hours later, with only Donna, Ken, Carole, and Gavin sitting peacefully on the Tandermanns' patio, exhausted by the exuberance of youth throughout the day. Lacy Sue and Saul took the twins home, with Mary following close behind. All were spent.

"Well. Let's raise a glass to youth," Carole said as she poured more wine in their glasses.

"Here, here," Donna countered. "I would love to capture some of it again, for sure."

There was a prolonged moment before a word was spoken, and it eventually came from Gavin.

"There's much to be said for youth, and its innocence. It doesn't have to struggle to capture its past," was all he said.

Donna and Carole glanced at each other. The two women, as usual, were in sync.

Donna observed Gavin for a moment before commenting. She noted a painful struggle in his features. "That sounds rather unlike you, Gavin. Are you having to capture your past?"

Gavin did not respond at first. Instead, he bent his head in a gesture of nodded surrender, before turning away, leaving the courtyard to return moments later. He placed upon the patio table a number of items, and then sat down, appearing disquieted.

Carole was the first to speak. "Were these items in the package you received the other day?"

He nodded. A pained expression crossed his face, and his eyes became teary. Carole reached to cover his hand. "What is it, sweetheart? What brings you so much discomfort? Please share."

In Gavin's silence, Donna, Ken, and Carole looked at the items on the table. Beside the items, Gavin placed a folder that was included in the parcel.

"I knew I was adopted at the age of three. My adoptive parents were British and treated me well. When I got older, they explained they had never really adopted me, but arranged for legal guardianship. It is why I retained my birth name," Gavin began.

"I spent most of my youth in Great Britain in a good home, with plenty of food, and an excellent education in a private school. Against the advice of my parents, I came to the United States when I was nearly twenty years old. That's when I decided to pursue a career in law enforcement. My British parents never spoke of my birth parents. I assumed all these years they knew little about them. Of that, I am still somewhat certain. Until yesterday, I never knew where I was born. I didn't even remember I had an older sister and younger brother."

"What?" Carole questioned loudly. "My goodness! Where are they now?"

Gavin grew quiet before answering. "They are dead." He grew still again before continuing. "The irony is they both lived in the

United States within a four-hour drive of me, and yet I had no idea. My older sister, Ida, six years older than I, died two weeks ago. My brother, Carl, two years younger than I, died a year ago."

"Oh, Gavin," Donna responded. "What a twist of fate."

Gavin, for the first time, lifted his head and looked directly at Donna. She shivered at his glare.

"It wasn't a twist of fate at all, but a purposely contrived plan. The package delivered to me contained a letter from my older sister, Ida. She admits she knew of my existence and where I lived, but made no effort to contact me or my younger brother all these years. Now they are both gone."

"Surely she must have had her reasons," Ken countered gently, concern for his friend evident in his voice.

With a measure of pride, Gavin looked squarely at Ken before answering. "Ida explains our biological parents were Jewish. This I already knew. We lived in Germany. This much my British parents shared."

Donna quickly did the math in her head. "You and your family were German Jews during Hitler's regime," she stated soberly.

"It would seem so. My sister provided an introduction. May I read it?" Gavin questioned.

"By all means," the group responded in unison. Carole moved closer to Gavin in a gesture of support, her eyes fixed on his facial expressions as he read. Ken and Donna held hands during Gavin's reading.

Dear Brother:

My English, after all these years, is poor. I have a dear friend translating my communication. I suspect you will be both surprised and disconcerted by this delivery. My wish is for you to conclude my actions and distance all these years were not meant to hurt you, but to allow an understanding. I am pleased to know you have found a profession and love in your life.

We had a younger brother, Carl, but he too is gone as of last year. I took great pleasure and comfort in knowing you and Carl were near. The years have not been kind to us.

For me, I was lucky to have eventually discovered a love in which I found a measure of healing. That is all anyone could wish for under the circumstances, along with the consequences. I deeply regret so much has been lost between us.

The enclosed will address most of your questions, and hopefully sedate your anguish. It is all I have to offer in these remaining days.

Your sister, Ida Tandermann Schmidt, Greenville, South Carolina

"Greenville?" Carole questioned with an incredulous tone. "*Greenville?* She was not more than four hours from us!"

"It would appear so, and yet she chose to stay distant," Gavin replied, his tone laced with sadness.

"What about your brother, Carl?" Ken asked quietly, not wishing to add to Gavin's discomfort.

Gavin's eyes became moist with emotion before he spoke. "I've been researching this since the package arrived. I did an internet search for a Carl Tandermann in North and South Carolina, given the fact the letter said we were all near.

"I found a 'Carl Tandermann' who died thirteen months ago. He lived in Raleigh, North Carolina. He was seventy-seven when he died."

"He was so close," Donna said in a subdued tone. "Oh, Gavin. This must be so painful for you. Your sister, Ida, how old was she when she died?"

"The records in the package support she was six years older than I."

Donna did a quick calculation in her head. "That would make her eighty-six. Surely she must have family in Greenville. Your brother, Carl, may have family in Raleigh."

"I have not had time to research this yet."

"What are these other things?" Ken asked, looking at the items Gavin spread across the table. It included a striped cloth with a star of sorts sewn upon it, along with an oval-type pouch with a drawstring that contained a small worn metal cup, spoon, comb, and sewing needle. All had an aged look. There were also two handwritten lists. The one list comprised numbers, twenty of them. The other list was titled *Kapos*. This list had nearly forty names.

"Who are these people?" Donna asked, perusing the list of names. "What are the numbers all about?"

"I don't know."

Donna, sensitive to Gavin's quandary, reached across the patio table to place her hand on his. "How can we help, Gavin?"

He was slow to respond, his eyes once again moist. "Give me a day or two. I simply don't have an answer."

CHAPTER THREE

"I have tried to keep memory alive. I have tried
to fight those who would forget. Becausee if we
forget, we are guilty, we are accomplices."

Elie Wiesel, Nobel Peace Prize Acceptance Speech, 1986

September 1939 – The Netherlands

Upon receiving the news, a look of anguish crossed her mother's face. Ida did not understand its implications until sometime later. Her father, too, had the foreign look of one undone by circumstances out of his control. They had crossed the German border into Holland after a two-day journey. As a family, they gathered at the train station at the proper time, according to instructions. Apparently there was a clerical error and Ida, the eldest of the three children, would not be getting on the train. Only her two younger brothers, Gavin and Carl, would make the journey. Her parents were assured a correction would be made as quickly as possible to address their daughter's transport. The plea was to be patient, but patience was in short supply. Many were mindful of menacing threats and rumors.

Ida's parents had heard about the transport and wanted it for their children. It afforded a way to safely exit before the borders closed. The gossip circulated, spawning a justified fear. Families were already lining the train tracks when they arrived, their faces etched with concern, all willing to compromise the family structure for the sake of their children.

Ida, along with her parents, said goodbye to her younger brothers, putting up a brave front for their sakes. She watched as her father ushered her brothers by the hand to their seats on the train, and told them to stay there until someone came for them. He assured them they would all be reunited shortly. He kissed each, and held them tightly before taking his leave just mere seconds before the train started its journey down the tracks.

Her young eyes saw her parents' bravery as a sham at best. Her mother fell to her knees on the platform, breaking down in uncontrollable sobbing as the train moved away from them. In her father's attempt to console and support his wife, he could do neither, and quickly joined her in her agony. Ida stood alone, watching the two strongest people in her life succumb to utter despondency and wondered why. She would never see her brothers again.

Shortly thereafter, her father settled their remaining family in the Netherlands, thinking it a safer haven. Within eighteen months of her two brothers' departure, however, the three would find themselves, as well as others, in hiding, taken in by Dutch families. A cruel and inhumane tempest overtook the Germany psyche. The Dutch people were alarmed to learn the now-ruling Nazi party was determined to make Holland *judenrein*—clean of Jews. In line with that resolve, the deportation of Jews to concentration camps accelerated. The family was safe for a time, but not for long.

⟨❦⟩

Present Day: South Carolina

Several days later, after the twins' birthday party, Carole noted Gavin placed the items that came in the package on a small table in his office. She looked intently at each item, and understood intuitively what she was looking at. Adding to the mix were stories from her youth by her Jewish parents. Waiting for an appropriate moment, she bided her time. While washing dishes after dinner the next evening, Gavin came up behind her, enfolding her in his arms from behind while her hands were still in dishwater.

She smiled to herself. "Are you back?" was all she asked, with a soft tone.

He didn't respond at first. His hold on her simply tightened to a degree she perceived as an affirmative, underscoring their deep connection. "I don't know. I only know you have been my constant family and the only family I have known all these years until we adopted Lacy Sue and Saul and the children."

Carole at once dried her hands and turned into the welcoming embrace of her husband. "Now and forever, sweetheart. It has always been my mantra when it comes to us. Now and forever."

Gavin nuzzled her before responding. "I never meant to shut you out. It's just the delivery of the package rattled my world. I thought I knew who I was, but now I don't."

Carole, short in stature but long in might, responded lovingly. "You are my husband, and the grandfather of three beautiful grandchildren, and my best of friends. That's who you are. We can deal with the rest."

Gavin melted further into Carole's embrace. "You have always been my strength and my fortress. How was I so lucky to have you by my side all these years?"

They held each other's embrace for a time, Carole grateful her husband appeared more himself again.

She thought for a moment before continuing. "I do have a thought, however, on the items. Would you care to hear it?'

"Yes, of course."

Carole led Gavin by the hand to the small table in his office where she had perused the items earlier in the day. "I have an opinion. It's not pretty. Hear me out."

"Tell me what you think. If I can't trust you, I can't trust anyone," Gavin returned softly.

Carole gazed at the items once again before looking at her husband, still holding his hand. She pointed to the first in front of her. "This cloth, the one with the stripes and the star. It appears to have been separated from the original garment."

"What about it?"

"It may be a remnant, a reminder of a category among prisoners," Carole said, looking all the while into Gavin's eyes.

"What prisoners?"

Carole tightened her grip on her husband's hand. "Holocaust victims, my love," Carole returned softly.

She waited for the full effect of her words to register. At first, his face revealed nothing. Carole continued to watch her husband's features, until finally, he appeared to grasp the meaning of what she had suggested.

"My sister?" he asked quietly.

"This may be what she is trying to tell us," Carole said. "The items in the pouch, the cup and spoon, may be from that time. I am simply guessing, but it bears considering the possibility."

Gavin slowly assimilated his wife's words before responding. "In a concentration camp? Are you suggesting my sister was in a concentration camp?" Gavin asked in growing agitation.

"I am simply offering the possibility. The striped fabric with a star and the pouch with a cup and spoon seems to be consistent with that."

"How would you know this?"

"The history of Jewish persecution is well documented, especially during the term of the Third Reich, Gavin. There are documentaries and movies galore. My family is Jewish. My own parents spoke of the time. Gavin, you are Jewish as well. Surely the time frame of your birth would fit with the items in this unexpected package," Carole ended, sounding more confident.

Gavin paced back and forth, absorbing his wife's words. His face seemed like that of a man piecing together long-ignored subtle clues that had nipped at his psyche for years.

He suddenly stopped, and turned around to face his wife. "My family members were victims of the Holocaust. Is that your position?"

Carole took a step forward to embrace her husband, placing her head against his chest. "My position, dear heart, has always been and will always be to love you to the end of time. In between, I plan to support you in every triumph, celebration, disappointment, and crisis. The rest is up to you. I will always be your champion. Still, the contents of the package would suggest your sister is, I mean, *was* trying to convey something. She was trying to tell why you and she were separated."

Gavin's eyes teared. He enfolded Carole in his arms, kissing her softly, his ability to draw comfort from holding her evident in their prolonged embrace. During the night they held each other in a simple, but reverent display of devotion. In this embryonic processing stage, Carole sensed her husband was imagining a past that, up until now, had escaped him. It was only through a fortunate turn of events that he realized a completely different experience from having been adopted. There was no doubt in her mind he would come face-to-face with the other side of his childhood, as well as that of his sister.

Carole's cell phone rang early the next morning. It was Donna.

"You are up before seven o'clock! This is a red-letter day! What is it that finds you crowing with the chickens on your day off?" Carole asked, jokingly.

"Good morning to you, too. To answer your question, Gavin's package woke me up with the chickens. I couldn't sleep a wink last night. That parcel has me a bit unnerved. What do you make of it?"

Carole knew her friend well. Donna was highly perceptive and even intuitive. "I think Gavin got a jolt from his past," Carole offered.

There was an initial quiet before Donna spoke. "I agree. What is your take? I know you have one."

Carole smiled. It felt good to have a dear friend who knew you so well. "I suspect the items in the parcel are remnants belonging to a survivor from Hitler's concentration camps."

There was another prolonged silence before Donna spoke again. "Okay. If this is the case, how can we know for sure?"

"So you agree?"

"I'm not opposed to the possibility. The star on the striped fabric makes me wonder, but it also rattles my nerves. What do we know about Gavin's past?"

"Not much, I'm afraid. It was pretty much what he shared yesterday. He was raised by a British couple who took custody of him in 1939. He was three years old. The British couple who took charge of Gavin was kind to him and raised him well until he left for the United States at the age of twenty. He never went back to Great Britain. His adoptive parents were killed in a plane crash when he was twenty-five. There were no other children."

"So until you, he was all alone," Donna said.

"Pretty much. Yet, I like to think I have made up for things," she replied with a chuckle in her voice.

19

"In that respect I am certain, girlfriend." Donna paused again before she spoke. "I have an older German friend, though I haven't seen her for some time."

"And?" Carole prompted.

"Perhaps I can have her look at the items in Gavin's package. She is quite old now, but very sharp. Would Gavin agree, if I were able to arrange a meeting?"

"I don't know. The Gavin I've been living with since the package arrived is not the Gavin I have lived with for nearly thirty years. I will ask him and get back to you."

CHAPTER FOUR

"More people are oppressed than free."

Elie Wiesel, Nobel Peace Prize Acceptance Speech, 1986

April 1942 – The Netherlands

The pounding on the door in the wee hours of the morning left no time to dress before the door was broken down from the outside. At once, the home in which they were hiding was filled with soldiers who ordered the family harboring them into the streets, dressed only in their bed clothes. It was early spring, and the morning air was still frigid and damp.

Ida, along with her father and mother, was already behind the secret wall, but could hear the harsh tone of the German soldiers and their demeaning remarks. Upon reaching the sidewalk, the family encountered a large segment of their neighbors. They, too, were in their bed clothes, shivering in the cold. Roughly handled by the soldiers, the slightest hesitation or misstep would result in a blow across the back or a kick to the legs. The dogs strolling beside some of the soldiers were ever-nipping at the assembly, with little to no restraint by their handlers.

"It has started," Ida's father whispered to her mother. The young girl didn't quite know what he meant, but even still a chill that had nothing to do with the cold in their hiding place traveled through her entire body.

The family and their neighbors stood in the frost-bitten morning for hours. No one was allowed to speak or even move. Those who had to relieve themselves were forced to do so where they stood. Any who dared speak or ask a question were immediately bludgeoned. For those families whose children cried, the penalty was a blow to the parents. The effort to quiet the children would become all-consuming.

By noontime, a German officer spoke to the now demoralized group of Hollanders. "Those harboring Jews will be shot! Those protecting Jews will be shot! Do you understand? You may return to your homes. They have been searched. Your only way to freedom is to fully unite with the Führer! This was your first lesson. It is up to you whether there will be other lessons. They will be harder each time, I can assure you. Dismissed!"

Indeed, those found in hiding would find another fate different from those who hid them. The few found harboring Jews that day were shot instantly, in front of their now-assembled neighbors. It would be a pattern repeated with certainty. All knew the *Schutzstaffel*, more commonly referred to as the SS, will come again. It was only a matter of time. Upon dismissal, the assembled returned to their now-ransacked homes, more afraid than ever. The ordeal was just beginning.

CHAPTER FIVE

Present Day – South Carolina

Gavin reluctantly agreed to meet with Donna's friend, though Donna did not reveal the fact that their relationship had once been professional. The encounter was arranged to take place at the home of the woman's daughter and son-in-law to avoid the stress of a drive, given her now-fragile health. The family had graciously offered their home for the meeting once Donna explained the issue.

It was a Sunday afternoon when Gavin, Carole, Donna, and Ken pulled into the driveway of Herta Cohen's home. They were warmly greeted by Herta's daughter, Suzanne Seigel, and son-in-law, Joel. Escorted toward the sunroom in the back of the house, Donna greeted her wheelchair-bound friend with a prolonged embrace that was returned just as warmly. Herta and Donna engaged in a lively exchange, not having seen each other for nearly three years, mostly because of Donna's hectic travel schedule.

"You are looking very well," Donna said, holding the elderly woman's hand.

Herta glanced lovingly at her daughter before responding. "I'm in good hands with my dear daughter and son-in-law. I lack for nothing. I understand you think I might be helpful, though."

"Yes. Forgive me. I'd like you to meet Ken, my significant other," she began.

"Oh! I have heard much about you, and all of it good! You are as handsome as the good doctor described you," Herta said, with a sly and wily smile.

"Also, these are my good friends, Gavin and Carole Tandermann," Donna said by way of introduction.

Herta shook both their hands, but lingered a bit with Gavin. "You are the one who has received things in the mail," she said quietly, before letting go.

Gavin, clearly uncomfortable, simply stepped back. Carole came to his rescue.

"Yes, Gavin recently received a parcel with objects we do not clearly understand. Donna suggested you might be able to provide some insight."

Herta nodded. Carole took the items from the box and laid them on the coffee table in the sunroom. Herta wheeled herself over to the coffee table to look at the collection, picking up each object with a shaky hand to examine it thoroughly before returning it to its place on the table. Shortly thereafter, her shoulders slumped and her manner became far more subdued. With each item, a cornucopia of thoughts and memories spilled into her mind. She turned to Gavin. "What do you know of these?"

Gavin was slow to answer. "Not very much. I know they were sent by my now-deceased sister, a sister of whom I have no memory. I have learned from a letter she sent with them that we had a brother, also now deceased. I don't recall either one of them. This package was a complete surprise to me. I am struggling with identifying its contents, along with what they mean and why she sent it at this late date."

Herta nodded. "I am sorry for your confusion," was all she said at first. "I am always intrigued by the path of pain. In its inception it is often searing, then it often lingers for generations, seeking a path, always circumnavigating the human experience."

Gavin's face questioned the response. "I don't understand," he returned.

She turned to him with a knowing smile. "Not all actions can be understood. It just is. Humanity has not begun to capture the essence of action and reaction, and it's sometimes an enduring legacy."

"Are you suggesting I have an enduring legacy?" Gavin asked.

"I am suggesting you are the master of your legacy. Whether this dilemma remains enduring is ultimately up to you."

Gavin was struggling to keep up with the older woman. "How can I know its length when I don't even know its meaning?"

"Once you know its meaning, you can begin to take control of its length," Herta returned.

Gavin looked at Carole, somewhat confused. "I'm not following you. We were told you might know something about these items," he stated, gesturing toward the coffee table. "Perhaps we were mistaken."

The old woman didn't look up nor did she respond at first. When she did, her features betrayed her years, far older and worn. "The items are from an unspeakable time, a time of shame for the German people." She picked up the cloth with the star. Her speech was far more labored. "This item I have seen before. It is the symbol given to the Jews. It was sewn on their clothing in the ghettos, and then again, in the concentration camps."

She peered closely at the other items, picking up the cup, spoon, comb, and sewing needle individually, examining each one with a piercing eye. "These are items given to those who entered the camps. You had to be careful that they were not stolen. Many learned to carry them on their person at all times. Not having these items could mean your eventual death."

Gavin eyed the old woman intensely, already understanding the unspoken. "Are you referring to Hitler's time? Is that what you are saying? How would you know about this?" Gavin asked gently.

Her initial response was a penetrating stare. The question, unbeknownst to Gavin, unleashed a memory of untold misery.

Herta raised her head proudly, looking at her daughter and son-in-law before responding. When doing so, she simply rolled up the sleeve on her right arm in answer. Concentrating, she wiped away the heavy concealing cream she used daily. She held out her arm for the group to see, her eyes intent on her daughter. A number was tattooed on her thin-skinned arm: -062406.

Her daughter, Suzanne, gasped. "Mother! I had no idea! How could you have kept this from us?"

"It was not a time I wished to talk about," was all the old woman said.

"Which camp?" Donna asked gently of her older friend.

"Ravensbrück," was the reply.

"How long were you there?" Donna asked, placing her hand on the woman's shoulder. Donna was observing the reactions of Herta's daughter, Suzanne. Her facial response and body language revealed a complete ignorance of her mother's past. Shock was written across her face.

"Three years."

"How old were you?" Suzanne queried.

The response was slow, but clearly audible. "Eighteen years old," came the trembling reply. After a sigh, the woman continued, "I entered the camps at the beginning of 1942. We were liberated by Soviet forces April 30, 1945. Except for myself and my brother, Helmut, who was freed from the Bergen-Belsen camp by the British just two weeks before Ravensbrück was liberated, all of our family died in the camps."

The old woman grew quiet, withering from an onslaught of emotions before she spoke again with a trembling voice. "I represent the remnants of a generation who bore unspeakable horrors. For years, I have wrestled with the trauma brought about by the despotic actions of a few, influencing the outcome of the many. I look back and I see despite the incomprehensible how we as a people have survived. We have not only survived, we have prospered. Evil can only go so far before it is turned back by the actions of good. If this were not true, humanity would eventually burn itself out on the bonfire of good intentions."

She grew quiet again. Her daughter and son-in-law were now engrossed in a conversation incited by strangers. The old woman turned fully to Gavin. Reaching up to place her hands on both sides of his face, she drew him toward her. "There is a message here. Of that, I am sure. Pursue it, chase after it. Channel the intent. Truth can bring pain, but it can also bring incredible freedom. I can only guess your sister was in one of the camps. Though she is gone, her spirit lingers. There is something she wants you to know and understand. You must pursue that knowledge."

"Why would she choose this method?" Gavin asked, with more than a bit of frustration in his tone. "I am just now finding out she existed; and now, after her passing, she sends me on a pursuit of I don't know what. I don't understand the logic of this."

Herta looked deeply at her visitor. "You have two choices. You can go back to your former life and forget you were sent these things, or you can search for the meaning of them. One path is easy, the other difficult. The decision, in the end, is yours. No one can fault you for either choice." The woman released her hold on Gavin and looked at her daughter. "I wish to go back to my room to rest." Suzanne wheeled her mother to the bedroom, and then returned to her guests.

After expressing their appreciation, Donna, Ken, and the Tandermanns made their way to their vehicle. Suzanne walked them to their car. "My mother has refused to speak of her youth all these years. My father, before his death, gave us a hint, but until today I was not sure. Thank you for the insight you have given me today. It lifts the veil, so to speak."

"You really had no idea she was a camp survivor?" Donna asked, surprise lacing her question.

"No. This is the first time I have seen the tattoo. You saw her effort to hide it with concealer. That explains her long sleeves throughout the years, despite hot weather. This answers a great number of questions.

"Please understand. She has been a good mother to me and my sister, but there have been dark periods as well; times when she withdrew into a quiet zone. My sister and I would refer to such times as 'the hole'." Suzanne looked at Donna more intently. "How did you come to know my mother?"

Donna was beginning to understand just how guarded her client's secrets were, not even revealing them to her daughter, even going so far as to hide her camp number with concealer. "We became friends awhile back," was all she said.

"I don't understand," Suzanne said.

"You will have to ask your mother," was Donna's reply. "I can only answer your question with your mother's permission."

"There is no need to ask my mother. I did a search on you when I got your phone call. You are a psychiatrist. I can only surmise my mother came to you for counseling. Congratulations, Doctor. You are the only one who, until today, knew of her past," the daughter conveyed with a hint of exasperation.

Donna didn't respond for a time, but simply looked at Herta's daughter. "Quite frankly, Mrs. Seigel, this is all news to me as well."

"You didn't know?"

"No, but I believe some memories are so painful they can't be uttered, even to those one loves. I hope we have not disturbed her peace by our visit today, or yours. If there is any way I can be of support, please do not hesitate to contact me." Donna then entered the front seat of the vehicle.

The drive home was a quiet one, with each passenger processing their visit to the home of Herta Cohen and her family.

"Where do I go from here?" Gavin asked from the back seat to no one in particular as they entered the Tandermanns' driveway. Carole took his hand in hers.

Up until now, Ken was largely quiet, observing, but not interfering. Upon hearing Gavin's question, however, he responded after shutting off the vehicle. "Now Gavin, that's a strange question for a retired FBI agent," he said as he turned in the driver's seat to face the older man in the backseat. "The first rule in investigation is to go backward to be able to go forward."

"Kinda' like a *Back to the Future* sort of thing, Ken?" Carole asked.

"Precisely. The detective in us never dies, Gavin. If your decision is to pursue this matter, you must go backward. I'm not telling you something you don't already know. You may have family you never knew existed, nieces and nephews you have never met. Your sister's letter revealed she had love in her life. Perhaps that means she had a family. You might want to start there. Nothing may come of it, but you just may find family, and a connection. I can't see where you have anything to lose."

"Yes," Carole said, picking up where Ken left off. "You know you had a brother. It's possible he had a family as well. It wouldn't be hard to find out."

The wisdom of Ken's and Carole's words had an immediate effect on Gavin. He nodded, drawing in a deep breath, and letting it out slowly. Other than Carole, and the Larsons, he never had family. He had lots of friends, but no family. He had been alone after losing his parents. Completely immersed in his career, he avoided long-term relationships because of his constant travel schedule. If truth were told, however, he wasn't interested in a relationship. They seemed too complicated, and he wasn't much for complication. Until Carole. Carole was his beginning and his end, his Alpha and Omega, and everything in between. She took him by storm.

They met at a convention in Sedona, Arizona. It was meant to be one of those retreats where law enforcement personnel met with those specializing in the workings of the lawless mind. Carole, a psychiatrist, was the keynote presenter. Boisterous with laughter and wit, she mesmerized her audience with stories, anecdotes, and tales to bring home the psychiatric aspects of criminal behavior. Carole was wide open, daring, contemplative, and highly effective in reaching her audience. When she concluded her delivery, the audience rose to their feet in loud applause. Gavin found himself applauding enthusiastically as well.

Later that evening, at the farewell dinner, Carole was surrounded by attendees offering her their praises. Gavin held back, but eyed her from a distance. There was something very different about this woman, he mused. So taken with her, he found himself securing a place in a line of admirers moving in her direction. Suddenly she was in front of him, taking his outstretched hand in hers. Then the magic happened. Years later, he would claim he fell in love that very moment.

At the same time, something happened to Carole. There was an energy in the handshake of the tall, mustached FBI agent. He said little, but his gaze was piercing. He simply said "thank you" but didn't let go of her hand. Nor did she want him to. It was the melding of two souls who had been seeking each other.

He managed, at the end of the evening, to make his way to her again. She was still surrounded by a slew of admirers. Once he came into her view, however, she halted all discussion and advanced in his direction.

"I think we spoke earlier," Carole ventured.

He was awkward at first, until he took in her piercing blue eyes. "We did, I…" he faltered, not knowing what to say. He was so new at this, and she was so beautiful. He managed to find his verbal footing. "Are you free for a drink this evening?"

She couldn't know at the time his heart palpitated near its limits. She simply said, "I would love that. I have some post-convention issues to settle, but I can be available in thirty minutes. Can you meet me at the bar in the Sedona Room? Ask any waiter where it is." Gavin could not know her heart was pounding as much as his.

Thirty minutes later, she entered the Sedona Room. He watched her enter and noted she was alluring with every step. What was it about this woman who moved him to his core? He didn't consider himself very handsome. He was, in his opinion, an okay-looking guy, and accomplished by some standards. He hadn't had many women in his life. In fact, there had been very few. He was looking for substance, but found very little of it in his line of work and in the women he had dated. It seemed to him, at this late date, most of the good women were already taken, and he had whiled away his time in his career, never grabbing one on the way. After all, he was now nearly fifty years of age and had never married. There were times he considered settling for a relationship, but he was too pragmatic. The odds of success were not in his favor, and he didn't want the chaos which would surely follow. What chance, anyway, did a fifty-year-old man have in establishing a relationship of substance?

Carole scanned the room, spotted him, and took a seat at his table. She had changed her clothing into a more casual outfit.

In spite of her more laid-back appearance, to Gavin, she looked stunning.

"I've been looking for a place to hide," she said. "I hate conventions."

Gavin was taken back by her sheer honesty. "You could have fooled me. You looked very comfortable with your admirers."

"You see, that's just it. I don't want admirers. I want people to hear what I say and apply it to their practices and careers. The rest is all window-dressing."

Gavin was impressed by her candor. He would discover candor was Carole's hallmark. Motioning for the bar waiter to take their drink order, they also ordered tapas dishes to complement their drinks. For the next three hours, they talked like they had known each other for years. Carole's sense of humor and wit were infectious. For the first time in years, Gavin felt very comfortable with a woman, one of substance. From that point on they were an item, both deeply in love, and married within a year. Content and devoted to each other for nearly thirty years, the fifteen-year difference in age was of little consequence to Carole. She had found the man of her dreams.

They adopted Lacy Sue, Seth, and Mary Larson as family years later when the young couple was struggling to find their footing. Their "found" family was Gavin's source of comfort these past years, a form of connection unconsciously craved. Yet, he had unanswered questions that would haunt him at unexpected moments. He would wonder where he came from, who his parents were; whether he had siblings, aunts, uncles, or grandparents. The list of questions was endless. He made a valiant effort to cast aside the legacy of his unsubstantiated past. After all, he was blessed in love and family, more than he could say. Yet, now he was presented with an unexpected opportunity to find real blood relatives, a real connection to his past. Did he dare hope? Could he, at nearly eighty years of age, find a connection to his past? He was, even before he stepped from the vehicle, considering the possibilities. His mind was revisiting his unresolved questions. Why now? After all these years?

CHAPTER SIX

"No one may speak for the dead, no one may interpret their mutilated dreams and visions."

Elie Wiesel, Nobel Peace Price Acceptance Speech, 1986

January 1943 – The Netherlands

Ida's mother reached for a blanket, only to be punched across the face and ordered into the streets. The blow knocked her mother to the floor. Her father quickly gathered his daughter to his side, while assisting his wife to her feet. Their worst fears were realized. Their hiding place was discovered. The family hiding them had been taken away an hour before. It would later be discovered that a neighbor had betrayed them, not an uncommon occurrence given the fear generated and the ruthlessness perpetrated by the Nazis. It was seen by those with weaker minds and less fortitude, as the only way to curry favor with the SS.

Ida and her parents were herded onto a crowded cattle car on a train, one of many such cars already filled to overflowing, not with cattle, but with people. There was no shelter from the cold, no food, and no water. Those in the middle of the car were afforded some protection from the cold, as they were surrounded by other bodies. Those on the perimeter shivered through the plunging temperatures, many wearing nothing but the indoor clothing they had on when arrested. Few had overcoats or hats. Ida, her father, and mother, were without overcoats, hats, or shoes. Their placement in the middle of the cattle car saved them. They would spend the night huddled together. The continual addition of other victims being shoved aboard the already crammed container caused some to suffocate. If it weren't for the cold wind, many would have been overcome by asphyxia.

In the wee hours of the morning, before it got light, they felt movement. They were on a train, and its destination was unknown to them. They traveled like cattle for what seemed like hours. Ida leaned against her father, sleeping as best she could, and waking to sunlight. The first thing she noticed was the overwhelming stench. Proud and decent people were forced to relieve themselves, defecating where they stood. Ida had observed her mother crying at times. Her father's face was that of a man vacant of answers. Hunger and thirst wracked their bodies, but no one dared to voice their discomfort. No one was listening.

After two days, the train stopped. All were ordered off. It was morning. The temperature was now below freezing. Ida stepped over bodies in the process of disembarking from the train. She would later learn that those on the perimeter of the car died. She looked back to discover more bodies not moving. Her father pulled her away.

"Are they sleeping, Father? Do they not know we have arrived?" she asked innocently.

"We must look ahead, not behind, my daughter," he replied, his voice hollow.

Soldiers ordered all forward, beating anyone who faltered. Her mother was crying again. Her father held her hand tightly, his eyes betraying a fear she had never seen in him before. Ida was struggling to understand what would become of them. After some time, their advance was stopped. Before them stood a beautiful wooded area and a large lake encased in ice. Her heart soared.

"Are we to live here, Father? It is beautiful," she asked excitedly.

"Yes, my daughter Nature is beautiful, but sometimes the heart of man is not," he said.

She was puzzled by his reply. They were ordered to march forward again. Eventually they rounded a corner of the forest and came upon a large opening comprising buildings surrounded by, she would come to understand later, an electrically-charged fence, barbed wire, and a multitude of soldiers with guns.

"Where are we, Father?" she asked. There was no answer. She looked up to see tears streaming down his face. It was the second time she had seen her father brought to tears, and the sight was unsettling to her still young and innocent heart.

"Father, don't cry," she begged. "Surely they wish to protect us within the fence."

Still struggling with the cold, they stood for hours for processing. Soon Ida could no longer feel her feet and hands. Slowly all moved forward. A soldier of some authority dictated the direction each person should take. Ida's father was directed to the left. Her mother and she were motioned to the right. Ida ran to her father in anguish, only to be roughly pushed back to her mother by one of the guards.

"Father! You must join us! You are in the wrong line!" she shouted over and over again.

Her father simply moved forward, his head down, never looking back. She didn't realize then that she would never see her father again.

Her mother, openly crying now, pulled her back. "Quiet, *Liebling!*"

"But Mother, Father is in the wrong line. He needs to be with us!"

"Be quiet, my daughter!" her mother said harshly, in a tone she had, before now, never invoked. It made Ida afraid.

Years later, Ida would learn the area in and around the camp was confiscated by the Nazis. Isolated, close to railroads and highways, it was the ideal location for arriving and departing transports.

Mother and daughter were moved forward, and along with dozens of other females, found themselves entering a huge bath house. All were ordered to take off their clothing and to leave their suitcases. Naked, they were harshly directed into a tiled room where their heads were shaved. Soon after that, the doors were shut and barred from the outside. Within minutes, pressurized hoses were turned on the women for delousing. The stream of fluid burned skin and eyes, and many cried out in pain as the onslaught continued. The pressure from the fluid was so great it knocked Ida to the now-slippery floor. Her mother struggled to bring Ida to her feet, her own eyes tearing madly and her skin raw. Ida began to cry, more from the viciousness of the action than from the pain.

The hoses were eventually turned off and the doors of the tiled room opened. Soldiers entered, some eyeing the naked women with lust in their eyes and sneering smiles. Ida's mother, along with the other women, hid their bodies as best they could as they were shoved forward to another room where they all received clothing. Striped long-sleeved smocks were dispensed. The clothing was made of a thick, coarse fabric. Wooden clogs were dispersed with little regard for shoe size. All were then given a small, brightly colored cloth fabric with two superimposed yellow triangles producing a six-pointed star, along with a needle and thread. The order was given to sew this yellow badge onto the left side of the striped smocks. Ida would come to understand the yellow star would identify those in the *Judendurchgangslager*, or the Jewish part of the camp.

After soldiers inspected the sewed patches, the women were ordered to another room where they were given a metal cup, a metal spoon, and a comb. In addition, each was assigned a number. All were ordered to remember their number and line up so it could be tattooed on their right forearm.

Afterward, the women were roughly ushered to the outside of the building, where they gathered in a large plaza and lined up in rows of ten. Here the newly assigned numbers were called. The importance of remembering the number would soon be demonstrated. Anyone not answering when their number was called would be shot immediately.

"Mother! What did they do?" Ida asked, not believing her eyes, and beginning to cry again.

"Quiet, my daughter! They should not hear you!"

Ida began to shiver, more from fear than the near-freezing temperature. It seemed forever that she, her mother, and the other women stood for the *appell*, or roll call. Twice a day they would appear for roll call on the *appellplatz,* sometimes standing for hours until the SS officer was satisfied the count of prisoners was correct.

After completing roll call, the women were assigned to their barracks. The sleeping area, one of three such sleeping areas in the Jewish section for women, would accommodate nearly one hundred women in each sleeping room. Each room was filled with three-tiered bunks made of wooden planks. A mattress filled with wood shavings, a pillow, a sheet, and a blanket were provided. A single wash room was to be shared by all three sleeping areas, to be utilized by more than three hundred women sharing twelve basins and twelve toilets. The washing area was void of privacy. One communal room completed the barrack layout. Despite the fact construction of the camp was so new, it was dismal at best.

"Mother, can we sleep? I am so very tired," Ida whispered, afraid to be heard, but looking at their assigned bunk with longing.

"Not until we are told to do so. It is still early. You need to wait until you are told," her mother said gently so as not to upset Ida. Despite her brave front, Ida noted a tear streaming down her cheek.

It was lunch time. Ordered to assemble on the *appellplatz,* the women and children waited for their number to be called before going forward to receive lunch.

Ida observed as others before her put forward their metal cup to receive a ladle full of soup and then disperse to eat. Upon hearing her number, Ida did the same, receiving her only sustenance in two days. She stood to the side waiting for her mother. Eventually her mother joined Ida and they ate their watery soup in silence, watching the others, many of whom had been in this place much longer than they.

Ida finished her soup in no time. "Mother, I am still hungry."

"Hush, my darling. I can't help you. This is all we have been given and we cannot ask for more."

"Why not? Why can't we ask for more?"

My mother sighed deeply. "This is our life for now, Ida. It will not be forever."

"I don't understand, Mother. Why is this our life for now?"

Ida's question went unanswered. Her mother simply hung her head. The young one would grow to understand and keenly observe the sights and sounds around her. Her youth would save her. The women would often share some of their meager food supplies with the children in the camp. There were days when her mother would add a portion of her food to Ida's, when the hunger were not so great. Over time, however, she became alarmed at her mother's weight loss and the pale and shallow face that stared back at her, her mother's smock now much too large for her shrinking frame.

"No, Mother," she protested one day as her mother again shared her food with her daughter. "You must eat. You will get sick if you don't."

"If I get sick, dear heart, always remember your mother loved you."

"But you must not get sick, Mother! Who will care for me, then? Will I need to search for Father?"

Her mother did not respond.

CHAPTER SEVEN

Present Day: South Carolina

Four days after their visit with Herta Cohen, Donna received a phone call from Suzanne Seigel, Herta's daughter.

"Mrs. Seigel, it is so good to hear from you. Is your mother well?"

"Now that's the thing, and it is you I have to thank. Your visit somehow opened the floodgates for my mother, and for us as well."

"What do you mean?"

"She slept very soundly the night of your visit. An unusual occurrence, I might add. She is often wakeful during the night, walking the floor with her walker. I've come to expect it, as it has been like this for as long as I can remember. It drives my husband mad, but there is nothing we can do.

"The next morning, however, she was up bright and early. She found her way into the kitchen and prepared a scrumptious breakfast for the three of us. We were shocked. She hadn't done such a thing since my father's death ten years earlier, never even coming out of her bedroom until close to noon time. Each day my mother eats her lunch and returns to her room until the dinner hour. Conversation is often stilted or none at all. We concluded it was because of my father's death, but there had been many such absences throughout our childhood, so we were primed for such occurrences.

"I want you to understand, many attempts have been made to include her in our activities: movies, board games, dinner out, visits to the park, and even vacations. She refused. We eventually stopped asking. The only time she is engaged is when our children come to visit. Our children love their grandmother! Quite frankly, however, it is the mother my sister and I never knew! With them she is animated, alive, and witty. How is this possible? Why the about-face? Frankly, my sister and I have always felt shut out. Until your visit the other day."

"Please share, Mrs. Seigel."

"After breakfast she asked my husband and me to gather in the living room. It was then she truly revealed her past, all of her experience in the camps. Much of it was difficult to hear. Your visit was the first admission she was a Holocaust survivor. I must confess that, until her sharing, I had harbored some resentment. Finally knowing the truth has brought about a whole host of reconciled feelings toward my mother. I promised my dad on his death bed I would take care of Mom, and I meant it, but I must confess, my heart was only half-engaged."

"Now?"

"Now, I understand the distance, the moments when she was emotionally unavailable, and the dark moods. They were all a product of her experience in the camps. Knowing she withstood the experience and survived makes me immensely proud of her. I see her through a different lens. Does that make sense?"

"It makes perfect sense. In my field, Mrs. Seigel—"

"Please, call me Suzanne. I feel old when someone close to my own age calls me Mrs. Seigel."

Donna laughed. "*Suzanne* it is, then. Secrets are rabid in the human experience. It's the dark secrets that are most troubling."

"I agree. I believe my mother was a victim not only of her experiences in the camps, but the resulting toxic shame as well. You see, I studied a bit of psychology myself and I know there are two forms of toxic shame."

Donna was impressed. "Share what you understand, then," she invited.

"One form can be righteous, as in trying to be more than human or acting as if we are perfect and can do no wrong. The other form can be a shameful response by acting less than human. These ones see themselves as failures, often becoming the dregs of society, believing everything about them is flawed and defective."

"Your summary is right on, Suzanne. In which group do you see your mother?

"I believe my mother is of the second group…not that she is of the dregs of society, but more a belief that she is flawed and defective. Now I understand. Her exposure to conditions in the camps at such a young age did not allow her to process that the deficit was not with her, but with her captors. At some point, she may have internalized the experience as being one who deserved punishment."

"After all, the survivors were told they were subhuman and responsible for their plight," Donna forwarded.

"Yes. I see it all so clearly now. My mother witnessed violence and unspeakable behavior. And yet, she hid these facts from us all these years."

"Your previous comment revealed her prolonged periods of disengagement from the family," Donna commented. "This had a profound impact on you and your sister, I am guessing."

"If only she had talked with us years ago," Suzanne said sadly. "Things could have been so different."

"From what you describe, however, there's been a healthy exchange."

"It's been unbelievable. She even looks different, a little younger. She stands more erect and seems to have more strength. I notice she's not relying on her walker as much. She talks more. Her appetite has improved, as well. She even helps out in the kitchen preparing our meals. My husband commented just yesterday he's almost enjoying my mother being around. Can I ask, Dr. DeShayne, how long you have known each other?"

"Now it's your turn to call *me* by my first name," Donna invited. "Near six years. As I shared the other day, I knew nothing of her camp experience until our visit."

"Even with you, she was hiding," Suzanne returned.

"Yes, it would appear so."

"After what she's been through, I can't blame her for not trusting anyone. One fascinating thing she shared with us, however, is that she contributed to the effort to establish the Holocaust Museum in Washington, D.C. before its opening in 1993. Apparently, for a short while she helped catalogue many of the items donated to the museum and placed on display."

"She never told me!" Donna exclaimed.

"She suggested Mr. Tandermann's quest to understand the package he received would be better served by a visit to the museum. They may be able to help identify the source of the items, which camp they originated from, etc."

"What a good idea! I will surely share with Gavin your mother's suggestion."

"Please, Donna. Feel free to visit any time. I know your visit the other day meant a great deal to her. I'd like to keep the momentum going."

"I will. Would it be all right to call her on occasion in between visits?"

"By all means."

⊘

Carole and Donna had plans for lunch the next day. Carole called first thing in the morning. "Hey, girlfriend. Gavin will be joining us for lunch this afternoon. Does that float? He has some running around to do in the morning. I suggested he join us and meet us there."

"Of course it floats! I'm delighted. Perhaps we can convince Ken to join us as well. It's been a while since the four of us got together for lunch. It sounds like fun."

Donna and Carole were joined by Ken and Gavin at a trendy new tapas restaurant boasting various ethnic offerings. They sat in a circular booth toward the back of the restaurant. The décor was tastefully done, with warm colors, lighting, and wall tapestries throughout.

"I feel like I'm in Morocco," Carole quipped. "The menu choices have me going around the world!"

"The choices are endless. How about we get a variety of tapas dishes and all share?" Donna suggested.

They agreed, spending the next few minutes choosing eight different small dishes, along with soup and salad. They eventually pushed their plates away, full and more than satisfied by the delectable entrees. After ordering a small dessert platter for the four of them to share and coffee, Donna broached the subject of her conversation with Suzanne Seigel, relaying details of the dialogue between the two women.

When she finished, Gavin was the first to speak. "I noted she was a bit vexed as she led us to the car. I'm pleased our visit proved to be positive, Donna."

"If anything, Gavin, it was a triumph. Suzanne now understands her mother better, and Mrs. Cohen is a freer woman for having revealed her past to her family. I think it's a win-win."

"There are just too many damned secrets!" Gavin returned with a tone of annoyance.

Ken leaned forward. "You're still miffed your sister kept her existence from you," was all he said.

Gavin's face gnarled at first, and then he quieted. "Forgive me. I vacillate between anger and elation. Anger because I had family I never knew about and they are all dead, and elation I have family I never knew I had all these years living in close proximity."

Carole covered her husband's hand with hers. "You've had the proverbial wind knocked out of you, and you're simply trying to catch your breath. It takes time."

"Carole is right," Donna offered. "You are still processing. Allow yourself the swing in emotions. It's all part of the process of adjustment."

Just then their dessert and coffee arrived at the table. Donna waited until they were settled before continuing.

"Herta Cohen suggested to her daughter that a visit to the Holocaust Museum in Washington, D.C. may provide you some answers, Gavin," Donna said. She watched Gavin, and even Carole, closely for a reaction.

"You're kidding?" he returned, somewhat defiantly. "What could they possibly know about my sister?"

Donna was taken aback by Gavin's tone. She took a moment to stir creamer into her coffee before responding. "I'm not suggesting they *know* your sister, Gavin. It's the items and the lists that may reveal something."

"It's only a suggestion, my friend," Ken offered to diffuse the tension. "Quite frankly, the idea of touring Washington, D.C.

appeals to me. I've never been there, but it's on my bucket list. It would be fun if the four of us toured D.C. for a long weekend."

"That does sound like fun," Carole said.

Gavin turned to Carole. "This idea appeals to you?" he asked.

"Why, of course. We've talked about touring our nation's capital, but we've never done it. This provides the perfect excuse."

"We don't need an 'excuse' to visit, but if you want to go, then we'll go," Gavin returned.

Carole turned toward Gavin and boldly took his face in her hands. "Now listen, big fella'. We don't do anything without the other wanting to do it as well. So you're either *in* or *out.* Just so you know, I'm not going if you're not going. So there!" With that she planted a hard kiss on his forehead

He laughed long and hard. "How could I say no to the 'General'?" he quipped, returning the kiss to her forehead.

CHAPTER EIGHT

"I swore never to be silent whenever human
beings endure suffering and humiliation."

Elie Wiesel, Nobel Peace Prize
Acceptance Speech, 1986

April 1943 – The Netherlands

The camp was still under construction. Ida and her mother
were assigned to the gravel pits to hammer large boulders of
stone and granite brought across the lake into small pieces.
Numerous cabins were still under various phases of construction. Ida
learned these cabins would house some of the SS soldiers and their
families. The pristine setting in which the cabins were built was a
beautiful wooded area along the bank of the lake. As each cabin was
erected, her mother and she, along with others in their detail, would
create a graveled walkway from the cabins to the compound. The
work was backbreaking, with little opportunity for rest throughout
the day. Their work began at daybreak each morning, and did not
end until just before dinner and their return to camp. There was
then the never-ending *appell* before being dismissed to their barracks
for the night after receiving their dinner.

Ida began to worry about her mother. The older woman was
becoming weaker, not eating well, and was not used to hard labor.
Her life as a wife and mother overseeing a household did not prepare

her for the rigors of slave labor. And that is what it was—slave labor. Ida saw many around her die and she became fearful for her mother.

She came to comprehend their plight, however. The talk in the barracks was an education for her young mind as she struggled to understand the harsh experience. She learned Jews were being singled out and considered a blight upon the German nation. The Nazi party was intent on creating a pure Aryan race. To do that, they had to rid the world of Jews. Not only the Jews, however, but also the mentally disabled and ill, lesbians and gays, prostitutes, political dissidents, the poor, and Jehovah's Witnesses—who called Hitler the Antichrist—all of which were cordoned off in separate sections of the camp. These groups were considered inferior human beings and enemies, or a burden to the state. The burdens would be put to death. The enemies would be turned into productive laborers, essential to the German war effort.

The shortage of food caused each prisoner to exercise great care with the meager meals they were allotted, especially dinner when bread was served with potatoes in a watery gravy. It was not unusual to find maggots floating atop the soup. On rare occasions, vegetables and even meat were provided. Many would eat half their bread with their dinner, saving the rest for the morning. You were lucky, though, if your bread was not stolen while you slept. It was also not unusual for those who died during the night to be searched in the morning by the hungry scavenging for extra bread. Your shoes were not safe, either. Many awoke in the morning without their shoes.

So it went. Ida and her mother struggled not to stand out in any way, not to draw attention to themselves either among the guards, kapos, or among the other prisoners. Soon, an emotional indifference permeated Ida's being. She soon lost count of the days. Her constant scan for a sighting of her father became her entire focus. Then one day, she and her mother were again transported, this time to Ravensbrück. Their misery was just beginning.

Those outside the gates were struck with Ravensbrück's immensity and the sheer number of prisoners, all women. The conditions were more dismal than could be imagined. Over time, overcrowding forced nearly two thousand women into barracks built for two hundred fifty. Many lay on the floor without blankets. Lice and disease took many lives; Ida's mother one of them. She lasted less than six months after their transfer. Severely weakened by hunger, Ida's mother was unable to ward off the onslaught of disease.

Having no one now to comfort and support her, Ida somehow managed to survive. *Appell* was at four o'clock in the morning. Five hundred women stood in the latrine around three toilets with no doors before the hated roll call during which everyone had to stand until all were accounted for. Ida became a keen observer, committing each name and face to memory. Her young heart grew hard, unmoved by the suffering around her. She would spend the days of forced labor imagining all manner of revenge. At night she would yield to exhaustion, but her dreams would reinforce the images that filled her mind during the day.

In the spring of her second year at Ravensbrück, rumors were rampant of the approach of the Red Army and the Americans. Camp commanders were in a tailspin. Evidence of the existence of so many prisoners had to be hidden. In the wee hours of Saturday, April 28th an exodus from the camp began, but the camp was in confusion. SS guards were fleeing, changing into civilian clothes before doing so, hoping to be taken for fleeing refuges. Women prisoners were streaming out of the gates under the control of the remaining guards. Nearly 2,500 women were marched toward Malchow, another camp miles away in Mecklenburg. Any who lagged behind were shot and left by the roadside.

The Russians were a few miles away to the east. The Americans just to the west. The SS didn't know where to go with the throng of female prisoners. Ida later heard that some of those exhausted prisoners, ravaged by thirst and hunger, stopped to pull up grass to eat and were shot. For some reason, Ida was not on the march with the other women, but still in Ravensbrück. The camp was in disarray. She had enough presence of mind, and just enough strength left in her weakened body, to enter the SS commander's office. It was empty; abandoned by SS soldiers fleeing in the face of the approach of the Russians and Americans. It was obvious that some attempt to destroy records was made, but abandoned.

Ida stood observing the chaotic scene, records strewn everywhere, just short of the incinerator. She gathered her strength and searched and then searched some more. At last she found what she was looking for. She retrieved several large folders that would serve her purpose. Hiding them in her dirty and putrid smock, she walked toward the *appellplatz* and waited for her liberation. Her energy was spent; she could go no further. Hundreds of other women were doing the same, too weak to move. Many died during the wait, just hours from liberation.

During this time, Ida allowed herself to think of her two younger brothers, Gavin and Carl. They had no idea what had become of their family, of the despicable renderings of a government gone mad. She took solace in the belief they were safe and hoped they were thriving in their new environment. Memory of their childhood play, teasing and laughter, would sustain her through a lifetime of choices. In the end, it saved her sanity, reminding her of saner days, of days spent with her dear family, enjoying childhood pleasures without a care in the world. Those memories were her mooring in the midst of unspeakable madness and would become her lifeline.

Years later, she would learn her siblings were separated after their arrival in Great Britain and taken to British families willing to harbor them. As far as she knew, neither one knew of the other's existence, or of the rest of the family that stayed behind. Her brothers were much too young to understand. Treated well, having enough to eat, and receiving an education, they, in the end, were the lucky ones.

Ravensbrück was liberated by the Red Army on the 30th of April, 1945 and turned into a refugee camp. Days after the liberation, Ida found herself, along with hundreds of other women, under the care of nurses and doctors. Five hundred prisoners were handed over to the Swedish and Danish Red Cross. Another twenty five hundred prisoners were eventually set free, being rendered well enough to travel. Ida was one of them after six weeks of recovery. She had no one. Where was she to go? Having time to think while recuperating, she had occasion to talk with some of the other women during this time. The conversations took on a life of their own, an understanding, a purpose, and then a clear resolve materialized.

The talk was quiet and protected, confined to a few. Brief discussions determined those admitted to the fold. One had to be focused, determined, and willing to give her life to the objective for as long as it took. There could be no wavering, no second thoughts, or excuses. Full commitment was paramount to success. Loyalty to the objective trumped personal issues. The group met again. And again. And again. Finally, the participants were condensed to those with a single-minded purpose, who would stop at nothing until justice was served. They would become a sisterhood for the rest of their lives.

The sisters would sometimes question, in the ensuing years, whether or not they had taken on the persona of madness. The answer would be *No!* They would conclude that their reasoning was correct. The circumstances would shift, the day would be adjusted, the method would change, but they would achieve the desired result, time and time again, without fail.

There would be an encounter early on, however, another twist in the form of an unexpected challenge. It tested the souls of the sisters. In the end, they decided to do the right thing. They gathered to assess the situation, determine their mission, understand the risks, and manage the outcome.

CHAPTER NINE

Present Day – Washington, D.C.

Ken, Donna, Gavin, and Carole landed at Reagan National Airport, in Washington, D.C. after a smooth flight. They checked into the Mandarin Oriental Hotel on Maryland Avenue and, upon the recommendation of the desk clerk, had dinner at a nearby Asian restaurant. They were not disappointed. The food was superb and the service top notch. Over after-dinner drinks, they discussed the following day's agenda.

"We are pretty much within walking distance of the 'must-sees'," Ken said, reviewing his map. "The Smithsonian, National Museum of American History, the United States Holocaust Memorial Museum, along with the Vietnam Memorial, and the new National Museum of African American History and Culture are all nearby. The choices are endless."

"Our main objective is the Holocaust Museum," Donna interjected. "Gavin, are you still agreeable to this?"

Gavin looked at Carole before responding. "I need to get this monkey off my back. Yes, we need to include it."

"Listen. Why don't we make it the first stop on our list, and then spend the rest of our stay on the other museums? That way, if we think of other questions, we can always return there before we leave," Carole suggested.

"Great idea," Ken said. "Tomorrow morning we head for the United States Holocaust Memorial Museum."

The next morning was overcast, much like Gavin's spirit. Carole noted her husband's mood. "We don't have to do this," she offered quietly placing her hand on his. "We can just do the other museums."

Gavin looked intently into his wife's eyes. "I thought of that. I sure did, but here's the thing. I'm not going to feel any better not having answers. So, as reluctant as I am, I need to press forward. I need to know my past. God! I'm nearly eighty years old and don't know who I am! I need some satisfaction before I die."

Carole produced a twisted smile. "I thought all this time *I* was the satisfaction," she replied with a devilish wink. "Go figure."

Gavin laughed heartily. His wife was always the wise-cracker, the one to bring humor to any situation. She was not failing him now.

"You *are* my satisfaction, my dear, and have been for all these years," he confirmed with a hint of seriousness. "You have always been my beacon. Even now, when I don't know my past, I always knew my future because of you. I was blessed the day I met you. I have never once questioned my choice."

"Then, dear heart, we need to explore your past. You and I, together. Game?"

He looked lovingly at his wife, moved by her devotion, and simply said, "Game!"

The two couples arrived at the United States Holocaust Memorial Museum, located within sight of the Washington

Monument. Considered a living memorial to the Holocaust, the building was an imposing four-story stone structure accented by a semi-circle stone entrance with three impressive openings that serve as a portico for visitors before entering. The center opening bore a large sobering banner bearing the words, *NEVER AGAIN – What You Do Matters.*

Donna had done some research on the museum, and filled them in on some of her findings while the guys were taking photos.

"The museum was commissioned and approved by Congress in 1980. Land was set aside, and building of the 36,000 square foot memorial began in 1989. It took four years and $168 million to complete, including the exhibits and opened in April of 1993. Auschwitz survivor and Nobel Peace Prize recipient Elie Wiesel served as its first chairman. As of June 2016 it had hosted more 41 million visitors, the first of which was His Holiness the Dalai Lama of Tibet. Ninety-nine heads of state and 3,500 dignitaries from 132 countries have visited, in addition to 10 million school-age children. In 2015 alone, the museum's website was visited by more than 16.5 million people in 211 countries."

"Whew!" Carole responded, impressed by Donna's summary.

Ken and Gavin continued to take photos of the building and banner just as a school group approached, one of many such groups visiting that day. After being directed through security, all were pointed toward a counter where they were encouraged to randomly retrieve an identification card. They discovered each card identified a real person who lived during the Holocaust and his or her story. Some were Jewish, others were not. Some were children, others adults. Some survived. Some did not.

Ushered into a large elevator by a tour specialist, their attention was then directed to an overhead monitor in the elevator to view a brief film before exiting. All visitors were provided with directions for making the most of their tour. Everyone was encouraged to meet, at the end of their tour, a one-hundred- year-old Holocaust survivor sitting in the lobby for the day who would welcome their questions.

The elevator delivered the group to the fourth floor where a timeline of events was presented, starting with the political unrest prevalent in Germany before the rise of the National Socialist German Workers' Party (the Nazis), and Hitler's subsequent rise to power in January 1933. Ken, Donna, Gavin, and Carole went to the theater to see the film before moving to the floors below. The unfolding displays, presentations, and video testimonials throughout the building served as a powerful reminder of untold suffering, along with heroic acts of sacrifice, as well as expressions of gratitude.

They ended their tour at the Wall of Remembrance, sometimes referred to as the Children's Tile Wall. Located in a corner of the museum, the wall displays 3000 tiles painted by American children to remember the 1.5 million children murdered in the Holocaust. The four of them gathered in front of a wall studying the tiles and reading the inscription:

Only guard yourself and guard your soul carefully, lest you forget the things your eyes saw, and lest these things depart your heart all the days of your life. And you shall make them known to your children, and to your children's children. – Deuteronomy 4:9

"To think we are approaching the time when most of the survivors and eyewitnesses to this time period will no longer be alive," Donna said reverently, her voice almost broken by emotion.

"More sobering is the fact that genocide and threats of genocide are still taking place in parts of the world. I understand more fully the need for the banner outside... *NEVER AGAIN – What You Do Matters*," Ken said somberly. Gavin and Carole nodded their agreement.

"You brought the items from the parcel with you?" Ken asked of Gavin.

Gavin nodded. "I did."

"Now would be the time to ask about them, wouldn't you agree?"

"I suppose it would. Who would I see about it, I wonder? Perhaps the front desk?"

"Give me a moment." Ken walked away and spoke with a person behind the information desk. "They were very helpful," he commented upon his return to the three waiting for him. "There is someone on staff at all times who assists in identifying papers and artifacts. They told me there is an archives' desk on the second floor. It was suggested we head there."

They found the archives' desk just outside the bank of elevators as they exited onto the second floor. The gentlemen behind the desk was an older, distinguished-looking person, with a shock of thick, gray hair and square spectacles set upon an imposing nose.

"He could pass for Albert Schweitzer," Carole whispered to Gavin.

"May I help you?" the man asked.

"I hope you can," Gavin returned. "I have recently received these items from my deceased sister. Can you help me identify them?" Gavin placed the items on the counter.

"May I?" the gentlemen asked permission, before touching the objects placed before him.

"By all means," Gavin assured the man.

He glanced briefly at the striped fabric with the inverted star before placing it to the side. Picking up the pouch with the drawstring, he began examining it from all angles before placing it back down on the counter. Gently pulling it open, he withdrew the worn metal cup, the metal spoon, the sewing needle, and comb, placing them with near reverence on a thick, red-velvet placemat-size protector he retrieved from behind the counter. He then studied each item carefully, turning them over in his hand, fingering them with care. At one point he retrieved a magnifying glass to examine the cup and spoon.

Having completed his review of the objects, he turned his attention to the two handwritten lists. "Explain to me again, how you came to have possession of these items," he said, while making a sweep with his hand over the objects.

Gavin cleared his throat before responding. "As I said, they came in the mail, along with a letter from my sister, a sister I don't remember." Gavin fumbled with his overcoat before drawing out his sister's letter from an inside breast pocket, extending it to the man behind the counter.

"Forgive my manners. My name is Cecil. Cecil Ratzeweit." The man in spectacles reached across the counter to shake Gavin's hand. Gavin introduced Carole, Ken, and Donna before allowing Cecil time to read his sister's letter.

Upon completion of the read, Cecil looked up at Gavin while removing his glasses. "This is all very interesting. Tell me what you know so far. No detail is too small."

Gavin nodded in understanding. "A parcel came to me recently in the mail. In it were these items, along with this letter from my sister, Ida. I have since researched the public records and have obtained a copy of her death certificate, as well as that of my younger brother, Carl, of whom I have no real memory. I am struggling to understand what I'm to do."

"I understand," Cecil returned knowingly. Cecil took on a thoughtful look before he spoke again. "The striped cloth with the inverted star is, most assuredly, a remnant suggesting the wearer was of Jewish heritage and a concentration camp survivor.

"As for the metal cup and spoon, they bear markings of its origin. Do you see the small 'H' at the base of the cup, as well as the spoon?" he asked, while passing a magnifying glass to Gavin, pointing to the marking. "Most camp items of this nature were engraved with a letter indicating their origin."

"I hadn't noticed it before now," Gavin replied, peering closely at the two items with the aid of the magnifying glass.

"Most likely, this cup originated from Camp Herzogenbusch in the Netherlands. It is often referred to, though, as Camp Vught. Established in 1942, it was the only concentration camp outside of Nazi-Germany. The construction of the camp was not complete until the arrival of the first wave of prisoners in 1943. By September 1944, 31,000 prisoners occupied the camp, some for short periods, some for longer periods.

"As you may have determined from your tour of our museum, the Nazi Germany scheme involved somewhere between fifteen thousand and twenty thousand camps. The exact number remains unknown. Some were concentration camps, some designated as extermination camps, and others as transit camps. Amersfoort and Westerbork of the Netherlands were transit camps. Prisoners were housed in transit camps temporarily until transferred to other camps.

"I am guessing your sister was in Camp Vught, at least for a time. The pouch is homemade and not of Nazi issue, however."

Cecil then addressed the two handwritten lists. "I'm afraid I have no idea what the significance is of these two papers. With your permission, I would like to have them examined by one of our staff members who is proficient in these matters. Would you be agreeable to this?"

Gavin looked at Carole. She nodded approvingly at the suggestion. "Yes, that would be all right."

"You will have to leave them. However. I can try to have them back to you by the end of the day tomorrow, if you are willing to trust me with them," Cecil replied.

"By all means. We are seeking answers, and your willingness to assist is very much appreciated," Gavin said.

"Here is my card, then. Come back around four o'clock tomorrow afternoon."

They said good-bye and headed for the museum gift shop.

CHAPTER TEN

"Whenever men or women are persecuted because
of their race, religion, or political views, that
place must—at that moment—become the
center of the universe."

Elie Wiesel, Nobel Peace Prize Acceptance Speech, 1986

May 1945 – Ravensbrück (Germany)

It was time to leave the camp. Ida had recovered somewhat. Her belly no longer delivered the deep pangs of hunger, although never really full or satisfied. She was becoming sturdy on her feet from regular nourishment provided by the relief agency. Her hair was growing back. Given clothing and shoes to wear for the journey, she said goodbye to those she knew she would see again.

Anticipating this day, she had struggled with the decision of where to go. Family and friends were either dead or missing. Nothing was as before. It wasn't safe for a young girl to be by herself. The instances of rape and beatings were numerous. She had only one choice.

Ida walked for days, keeping out of sight as best she could, sleeping in the woods, in caves, or under rock formations. She begged for food along the way, but was not alone in this. Thousands of refugees clogged the roads in their struggle to return home, praying there was a home to return to. Many of generous spirit along the way would give her something to eat from their meager reserves. Others did not. Even now, some did not want to believe their leaders had been mad men betraying their country in unspeakable ways.

She lost track of time, putting one foot in front of the other as Ida advanced toward her destination. Finally, Ida detected familiar surroundings as she drew closer to town. Few people were on the streets of this once-bustling community. Those who were did not look up in greeting, but kept their eyes averted, as if frozen in fear. Many homes and businesses were boarded. Others looked abandoned or neglected. Dogs ravaged by hunger prowled the streets. Rat droppings were everywhere. The effect added to her foreboding.

Ida reached her destination. Here, too, the once-charming appearance had succumbed to a lack of attention. Her only solace was in realizing the building was not boarded up. Was it possible someone still lived here?

Hesitantly, she made her way up the stairs to the door and knocked, stepping back slightly after doing so. There was no answer. Perhaps she was wrong. Perhaps this home too was abandoned. She stepped forward to knock again, this time more insistently. Again, no response. She was about to turn away when she heard the sound of a lock turning, and then another, and still another. The door opened.

"You have returned, my child," the woman said, opening the door widely.

"I have no place to go," she told the woman. Thin and worn with sad eyes, Ida first thought she was looking at someone else. It was her, though, the woman who hid Ida and her parents from the SS behind a wall in her home. The same woman who had been caught and taken away.

"Then your home shall be with me for as long as you like," was all she said, ushering Ida into her home and relocking the door three times.

The interior of the house was just as Ida remembered. The woman, Ilse Kaiser, and her sister, Ella, had been meticulous housekeepers. They had lived in this three-story house with their father, Gustauv, for years before being taken prisoners by the SS. Neither daughter married. They sat at the dining room table.

Ida looked around. "Ella? Mr. Kaiser? Are they well?" she asked naively.

Ilse's eyes became teary. "They are gone. Father did not survive his imprisonment more than three months. I was told he took ill with disease. His age was against him. If disease had not killed him, the gas chambers would have. Ella died six months before my release. She held out as long as she could."

"You were all so good to me and my family. You were released?"

"A clerical error. I found my way back here. Four weeks later, it was ordered that those in the camp over the age of fifty were to be exterminated. I had just turned fifty when I was released. God works in mysterious ways." There was a pause before Ilse spoke again. "You are all alone now, Ida, as well?"

"There is no one left. I assume my aunt and uncle are gone as well."

"A story told over and over again, I fear. I have soup, child. You are hungry?"

"Yes, I am hungry."

Ilse went to the kitchen and returned to the dining room with a small bowl of bean and potato soup. It was delicious. "There is not much food. I have managed, since my return, to gather seeds and start a garden, but I haven't planted them outdoors for fear of theft as they begin to germinate and grow. My garden is on the third level. I will show it to you later. Flour for bread is scarce, but we can still get it. Meat is almost non-existent, and when it is available, one has to question the animal it was taken from. People are desperate and will do desperate things. We must never speak of the garden to anyone. Do you understand?"

"I understand. Do you live here alone?"

"A gentlemen who lost his leg in the war stayed with me for a time. He has recently left for Berlin. I questioned his decision. Berlin has been devastated, but he has a sister there who has taken him in."

"And the shop?" Ida asked, referring to the store below at street level. Gustauv Kaiser was a watchmaker. His two daughters assisted him in the shop.

"There is some business, but very little. People have other priorities, like survival."

Ida finished her soup wanting more, but hesitated to ask. Ilse returned to the kitchen, bringing back a half cup more, pouring it into her bowl. "We must conserve, but we must also celebrate your return."

Ms. Kaiser then took Ida to the third floor of the home to the garden. The whole level had been transformed into a greenhouse consisting of tables of vegetables such as beans and fruit in varying stages of growth. "We should have lettuce in another week. The windows provide enough sunlight. I struggle to bring water up the stairs, though."

"Perhaps we can run a hose. It will be easier. You have done all of this?" Ida asked with more than a hint of awe, mesmerized by the potential of enough food after years of want.

"It has to be this way, at least for now. I no longer trust my neighbors. It was one of them who betrayed us and you."

"Do you know who?"

"Yes."

Ida chose not to question further. She surmised that it would do no good. She looked across the room at the wall behind which she, her father, and her mother hid for all those months. There would be time. Time to right the wrong.

"How can I support you, Ilse?"

Ms. Kaiser smiled broadly for the first time. "I recognized you to be a good and caring child, Ida. My family was not mistaken by hiding you and your family. It was an honor to do so. I am pleased you found your way back to me. I need for you to attend to the garden. It is our lifeline. Germany has been ravaged. It will not be normal for some time. I'm afraid their leaders brought it upon themselves. The garden will sustain us until Europe finds its footing, by the grace of God. I can attend to the shop. Hopefully business will pick up and support us to a greater degree. For now, we will survive and then we will thrive. In the meantime, we must plan times of worship, as before."

Ida was shocked at the comment. "You still believe in God?" she asked incredulously. "After all you have seen and witnessed, you still believe in God?"

"Oh, my child! It is easy to blame God for man's inhumanity. It is not God who visited upon us such atrocities, but the Antichrist. If Christ is not supreme, then darkness rules."

Ida heard the words in disbelief, and spoke before thinking. "Forgive me, Ilse, for my lack of belief. From what I have seen and witnessed, your Christ took a vacation, and darkness set up housekeeping at the expense of millions of Jews and their families. I am not so ready to excuse his absence or indifference. Perhaps one day, but not today."

It was at this point, Ida understood the depth of her rage, a rage that sought an outlet. For now, she had shelter and would have food, along with a measure of control in her dealings. She was growing quickly, maturing to adulthood by leaps and bounds. There was work to be done. It started with removing the concentration camp number tattooed on her arm. The sisters had agreed this was the first step before meeting again.

The months passed quickly. The garden yield was plentiful, more than enough to preserve for the winter and to even sell. She and Ms. Kaiser gathered enough chickens to sell eggs, and enough milk to make butter. Flour was becoming more plentiful, so they made bread, selling items in the shop below. The chickens had to be fenced in to prevent theft of both the chickens and the eggs. They converted an outdoor shed for this purpose, locking it securely each time they entered and exited.

This went on for a time. People heard of their efforts and came to purchase vegetables, eggs, and baked goods. Some even wanted their watches repaired. A fragile stability was beginning to return to them personally, though the country was still in the depths of political and social upheaval.

Ilse, a devout Christian, organized a Bible study group in her home, meeting once a week.

"You are not attending our Bible studies, Ida," she ventured aloud one day several weeks after its formation.

Ida simply looked up at the woman who had given her shelter and protection, not wanting to offend. "It is too soon for me, Ilse. I haven't come to terms with your God who looked the other way while so many were suffering. Perhaps in time."

"I will pray for you."

Toward the end of fall, Ida announced she would be traveling to Berlin to investigate the whereabouts of her mother's sister. The trains were running again, though their service was spotty in places.

"Why Berlin?" she asked, obviously surprised by Ida's announcement.

"I understand there are records and postings of people who are trying to find each other. The relief agencies have set these up." This explanation was the best she could offer under the circumstances. Ida couldn't reveal the real purpose for her travel was to attend a meeting with the sisters.

"The weather is getting colder, and Berlin is still destroyed from the bombings. Wouldn't it be prudent to wait until spring when the weather is warmer and conditions are improved? Besides, it is not safe to travel alone."

Ida had rehearsed this conversation in her mind in anticipation of resistance to her idea. "I thought of that, but spring will require my full presence to ready the garden, and besides, if I wait too long, I may miss the opportunity to get such information. This is something I must do. I took the liberty of writing to Mr. Coble, the gentlemen who lost his leg in the war who stayed with you for a time. He assures me that I can stay with his sister. So you see? I will not be alone."

"Mr. Coble and his sister? My, you have thought of everything, Ida. I wondered why you wanted Mr. Coble's address. Now I see. I suppose I don't have the right to stop you, but I am concerned for your safety."

"I shouldn't be gone for more than a week. All the canning has been done, and the last of the potatoes won't be ready for harvesting until after my return. So you see, this is the perfect time to go."

"Yes, perhaps. You will come back?" Ilse asked with a hint of fluster.

"Oh, Ilse. Of course I will return. This, because of you, is my home."

"I can help with the train fare," the older woman offered.

CHAPTER ELEVEN

Present Day: Washington, D.C.

Gavin, Carole, Donna, and Ken woke early to get a good start on their plan to visit the newly opened National Museum of African American History and Culture on the National Mall. The cost of most of the four hundred thousand square foot museum, they would soon learn, was covered by donations and grants in its ten-year fund-raising endeavor.

They spent the day exploring the museum's elaborate multi-floor display of nearly 37,000 artifacts in its mission to relate the African American experience through decades of history, struggle, and victory.

"I am so glad we had sense enough to order tickets ahead of time. This place is mobbed," Carole commented.

"That it is. Our nation has proudly sponsored museums and monuments that tell our history, but has left out, until now, another poignant reminder of our past. This museum is brutal, exhilarating, and hopeful, all at the same time," Donna responded.

"Long overdue," Ken added. "The design is awesome."

Donna, ever the researcher, filled the group in on the museum's formation. "I had a chance to read about this. Apparently, this museum was the brainchild of Lonnie G. Bunch III, its current director. His passion as a scholar for filling in missing pieces of American history propelled him toward creating an expression for the up-until-now unspoken. The actual design of the building is credited to David Adjaye, a Tanzanian-born British architect. It is unlike any other structure in Washington, DC. Adjaye made extensive use of glass in an upside-down ziggurat, similar to design often used in Yoruba art in Nigeria."

"So this gentlemen brought Nigerian art to us," Gavin said, obviously impressed.

"It appears so," Donna responded

It was mid-afternoon, and they were mindful of their appointment at the Holocaust Museum. Having just concluded their tour and now standing outside the National Museum of African American History and Culture, Carole made an observation.

"Hey, guys. Do you see what I see?"

They all looked at each, shrugging their shoulders. One never knew Carole's angle.

"From where I stand, I can see the Washington Monument."

The group followed her gaze.

"Isn't it interesting," she continued, "that a monument to a slave holder who founded our democracy is right across the street from the National African American Museum. To me, that's karma."

The group walked from the National Museum of African American History and Culture to the United States Holocaust Memorial Museum at a rather fast clip to arrive on time for their appointment with Cecil Ratzeweit. Everyone was still digesting the morning's museum experience as they walked.

"Yesterday," Donna said, rather forlornly, "we visited the Holocaust Memorial Museum. Today, we visited the African American Museum. Both museums tell the same tale when you get right down to it. It's a tale of unspeakable horrors because one race thought themselves superior to the other. Slavery was part of both. I continue to be baffled by human reasoning. Regardless of color, race, religion, or ethnic background, the sum total is, we are all human. How is it that our combined history as a nation or as a planet, tells some a different tale? How some can be convinced they are superior or purer or somehow endowed with special position or privilege is beyond comprehension. We all bleed the same, we cry, we laugh, we give birth, we sicken and we die. We all need food, sleep, love, and comfort. The only difference lies in our skin color, language, and belief system. Yet, those aren't differences. Those are variety. All creation is composed of variety. Why is human variety treated differently? I went into psychiatry trying to understand the human psyche. I am still looking for the answers. It boggles the sane mind why humans, the same species of life, treat variety differently."

"You're preaching to the converted, girlfriend," Carole added. "You have seen for yourself the machinations a sick and distorted mind can produce. The rationale for those with sick behavior is, in the end, irrational."

"This is the effect these museums wanted to achieve when they were created. These types of presentations are meant to rattle us, to get us angry enough so we act to prevent periods of cruelty and insanity from happening again," Ken offered, "But did anyone notice there was little tribute given at the African American museum to Judge Clarence Thomas, a currently sitting black judge on the Supreme Court, and the second to serve?"

"I didn't notice," Donna returned.

"I didn't either," Carole said. "What made you take notice? Is that important?"

"I've been an ardent follower of the Supreme Court and its decisions for years. I just find it odd they took the time to display

Chuck Berry's red Cadillac, but did little to recognize Judge Thomas after serving twenty-five years on the Supreme Court. Perhaps it is Anita Hill's accusations at his confirmation hearings, however he is considered by many to be a heavy-weight as a legal thinker, although I understand he tends to be distant with advocates and his fellow justices at times, but his background is inspiring, nonetheless. I just feel the presentation is underwhelming."

"We're here already," Gavin announced as they neared the Holocaust Museum.

Heading straight to the second floor, they found Cecil waiting for them. "Follow me and I will take you to a small conference room down the hall. We will be joined by Kathe Hohman. Mrs. Hohman oversees German translations. Since your papers were in German, I asked her to review her findings, if any, with you."

As they entered, an elegantly dressed elderly woman was seated at the table. She rose to greet the group. "I'm Kathe Hohman," she began, extending her hand to each of them. "I have the honor of being head of the German translation department for the museum." Mrs. Hohman's manner was warm and engaging.

Cecil singled out Gavin. "Kathe, this is Mr. Tandermann. He is the gentlemen who brought the papers, and the other items."

"Let's sit, shall we?" Kathe suggested to the group. "Mr. Tandermann, please sit by me."

Once everyone was seated, Mrs. Hohman turned to Gavin. "I understand the papers and these other items were sent to you recently."

"Yes," Gavin confirmed.

"Cecil tells me he has identified the origins of the cup and spoon from Camp Vught. The letter from your sister is intriguing to say the least. It makes one think there is more to this communication."

"In what way?" Gavin asked.

Kathe picked up the letter and pointed to it. "Notice she says her absence, was to 'allow an understanding.' Further on, she comments on 'circumstances, along with the consequence.' That kind of veiled wording, Mr. Tandermann, was purposely done in the hope of further investigation. I am almost certain of this.

"Now, Camp Vught housed both men and women, segregated in their own sections. Many in the women's section were eventually transferred to the Ravensbrück concentration camp about fifty miles from Berlin. It holds the distinction of being the only major women's Nazi concentration camp.

"As you may have learned from your tour of our museum, all concentration camps, and extermination camps, were under the control of Heinrich Himmler, head of the *Schutzstaffel*, commonly referred to as the SS. Himmler is considered the main architect of the Holocaust, the Nazi's program to achieve the objective of a pure, German blood line.

"I have looked at the archives related to Ravensbrück. When the Red Army was nearing the camp, the Germans attempted to incinerate as many records as they could to hide their actions. They were largely unsuccessful. The SS was in turmoil and command in the final days and hours of the camp was spotty at best. Even so, the SS attempted to transfer the archives of the camp to a safer place. As a result, many records were found and preserved. Of special interest is the list of prisoners, more than 132,000 women and children who were incarcerated."

Kathe Hohman stopped her summary and looked at Gavin. "Mr. Tandermann, there is an Ida Tandermann listed in the prisoner archives of Ravensbrück. She was nearly thirteen years old when she entered the camps. Her mother, Hinkle Tandermann, died in Ravensbrück. Her father, Olaf, died in Camp Vught. There are no other children mentioned as related to Hinkle or Olaf Tandermann."

"I don't understand. What are you suggesting?" Gavin asked, his face now pale.

"Where were you raised, Mr. Tandermann?"

"Great Britain. I was adopted. I came to the United States when I was twenty. What does that have to do with my sister?"

"It is possible, and even probable, that you and your brother were part of the Kindertransport project. It would explain your separation from your family."

Gavin looked at Carole. She reached for his hand.

"You may wish to go back through the museum to find information, displays, and artifacts related to Operation Kindertransport. It is located on this floor. It would make sense that you and your brother may have been two of the 10,000 children ranging in age from infants to teenagers who were transported to willing families in Britain who understood the evil intent of the Nazi regime. It was no small gesture on the part of the British people, who raised half a million British pounds in six months for the care of rescued children given shelter in farms, hostels, and private homes in Britain. It is possible two separate families accepted responsibility for you and your brother. Your parents fully expected this arrangement to be temporary. Sadly, in far too many cases, it was not."

Donna leaned forward. "How can we know for sure?"

Kathe looked at Gavin and then at Donna. "Records of the children can be obtained at the World Jewish Relief Organization, a British Jewish charitable agency. You can possibly do an online search. Thankfully, Sir Nicholas Winton, credited with heading the effort to transport the children in 1938, kept meticulous records. His story is worth exploring. Mr. Tandermann, you have copies of your birth certificate, I assume?"

"I do not have my original birth certificate, but I do have a certified statement."

"One more question. Do you know who sent the parcel? Was it your sister? Or was it someone else? Perhaps a family member you have yet to meet? You may also explore where your sister lived after leaving Ravensbrück. At times, the relief agency handling the refugees required a forwarding address."

"I understand," Gavin murmured.

"What about the two lists? Have you been able to determine what they are about?" Donna asked, fully engrossed in the discussion.

"Not to my satisfaction. If you remember, the one list is comprised of numbers, twenty of them. That tells me nothing."

"For some reason, his sister wanted him to have the list, so it has to be significant," Carole interjected.

"I would agree," Kathe returned. "The other lists, however, is titled *Kapos*. This I find interesting. It is a list of names, nearly forty."

"Who do you think they are?" Gavin asked.

"Let me explain. In the camps there was a strict hierarchy. The camp commander and his staff were at the top. Ravensbrück was commanded at first by Max Koegel, the first commandant, who was replaced with Fritz Suhren. Suhren, in my opinion, was the more evil of the two. Below the camp commander are the SS guards and other SS support personnel.

"On a daily basis, however, prisoners had to answer to the kapos, who themselves were prisoners, appointed by the SS to supervise the work and behavior of their fellow prisoners."

"In return for what?" Ken asked, with a note of annoyance. "There had to be a payoff."

"The kapo system, enacted by the SS, was the very heart of the camp. It provided for staffing, thus saving money and helped to control the vast numbers of prisoners. In return, the kapos would receive extra consideration. Perhaps more food, convenience, and privileges. For those prisoners, it was a way to survive."

"So why is there a list of forty of them?" Carole asked.

"I cannot answer that question," Kathe returned. "It remains a mystery."

The meeting ended with an appeal from Kathe Hohman. "Clearly, Mr. Tandermann, your sister, for whatever reason, chose not to engage with you, even years after her camp experience, all the while knowing where you lived. This haunts me. Please promise to contact me should you discover the reason."

"I will certainly do so," Gavin assured the woman.

Gavin, following his wife and friends through the door, stopped and looked back at Kathe Hohman. "Forgive me, Mrs. Hohman, but I need to ask. How is it you know so much about the camps?"

Nodding a dignified acknowledgement of the visitor's question, she smiled slightly, and then rolled up her sleeve to reveal a tattoo; a number: 051853.

CHAPTER TWELVE

"There may be times when we are powerless to prevent injustice,
but there must never be a time when we fail to protest."

Elie Wiesel

November 1945 – Berlin

I da arrived safely, but the journey was arduous. The closer to
Berlin, the more the displacement of rail service. Upon exiting
the train, she was shocked by the devastation wrought upon
the city by Soviet and Allied artillery shelling. She had to remind
herself Nazi Germany's downfall was just six months before. Rubble
and ruin stretched as far as the eye could see. People, hungry and
huddled in the streets, having no place to go, were thankful for any
warmth they could muster. Small fires were burning on the streets
with people sitting around them. The hunt for wood was an ongoing
necessity.

Rumor was rife concerning the closing days of the Nazi empire
in this once beautiful and cultured city. While Hitler hid away in an
underground bunker, the Soviets surrounded the city and waited for
the command. On April 20th, Hitler's birthday, they began shelling
the city. Over the next twenty-four hours, the Red Army's noose
tightened, despite the presence of 45,000 inhabitants.

German soldiers, most of them young boys and old men of the
Volkssturm, were sent to hold back the Soviet army and Allied forces.
Berlin was doomed, forsaken, and duped by its leader.

It had been another few days before Hitler committed suicide, signing his last will and testament before a hasty marriage to his long-time lover, Eva Braun.

The city, still in shock and denial, understood the country's civil and military structures had been decimated. Who would lead them now? The Red Army? The Allies? Little was available in the way of services; food, shelter, and medical care were almost non-existent. When it became safe, relief agencies had begun to move in to offer services.

She was met at the rail station by Sarah Sonntag, the sister of Rudolf Coble. It was an unexpected gesture she had not anticipated.

"It is not safe for a young woman to travel alone in our city," Sarah stated unequivocally, as she greeted the stranger her brother insisted on hosting because of the kindnesses afforded him through Ilse Kaiser. Sarah, a middle-aged woman, was lacking attractiveness in every sense of the word. Her face, distinguished by a big nose, close-set eyes, and decayed teeth, was accented by a tuft of dirty and unruly hair. Her manner and dress were bohemian, at best.

"I am most indebted for your thoughtfulness. Ms. Kaiser sends her warmest regards to you and your brother."

"We have little to share, I fear. Simple bedding is all we can offer. Times have proven difficult."

"I am grateful for your hospitality. I don't wish to increase your burden."

"You are here, if I understand, to determine the location of relatives."

"Yes, my aunt and uncle. They lived here in Berlin before the war."

"I wish you success in your endeavor. As you can see, Berlin is in turmoil. It was once a beautiful city, the center of youth and vigor. Did you know Hitler had commanded his Minister of Armaments,

Albert Speer, the architect, to transform Berlin into a shining city after the war? The architectural plans for Berlin were without comparison, and became the Führer's pet project. If realized, the entire city would have been recognized as a monument to the Nazi effort."

"I didn't know of such plans," Ida said feebly, unable to feign interest.

"The transformation of Berlin into the Welthauptstadt Germania— or world capital of Germany—had already begun. The Berlin Olympic Stadium, used for the 1936 Summer Olympics, was the first project. Then came the new Chancellery, and its vast, stately hall. It is now in ruins, I fear. The grand culmination for the Welthauptstadt, however, was to be the Avenue of Splendours, a five-kilometer-long boulevard serving as a parade ground and completely closed to traffic. Renditions of this were in the papers. It would have been a spectacular parade route." Sarah Sonntag appeared dreamy-eyed as she remembered, almost reverently, the plans for Berlin's transformation.

"The Führer planned for a World's Fair after the completion of Berlin's renewal, did you know this? Of course not. Forgive me for my insensitivity. It will never be realized. The change from vibrant city to one of desolation is heart wrenching. So many have been lost and unaccounted for. We continue to stumble over the ruins, seeking meaning, not to mention food. My brother and I are lucky we have shelter. I understand my brother was treated kindly by your Ms. Kaiser. We are grateful. In the midst of madness, there remains the sane and kind heart. It's likely, however, your aunt and uncle are no longer in the city. Many have fled. I pray the relief agency handling these matters can be of assistance."

Ida followed Mrs. Sonntag toward a dilapidated, partially bombed building. Climbing over a ruble of ruin before reaching a makeshift door, Mrs. Sonntag led Ida into the one-room shelter. The interior was dark, with a very small window allowing for a measure of light. There were straw-filled mattresses on the floor, similar to that of the concentration camp. A man was sitting on a small stool in the corner of the room.

"Rudolf, our guest has arrived," Sarah announced unceremoniously.

"This would be Ms. Kaiser's friend, I assume," the voice from the corner questioned.

"Who else would visit our deplorable shanty?" his sister returned.

"Mr. Coble, I am Ida Tandermann. I am grateful for your hospitality, sir," Ida offered feebly after her vision adjusted to the dimmed lighting.

Stunned by the surroundings, not much better than the camps, Ida made an effort to hide her shock. Fumbling in her bag, she brought out several jars of preserved foods from the garden. Upon Ilse's insistence, Ida agreed to her suggestion to pack these. She was now glad she had done so.

"I bring you gifts from Ms. Kaiser and myself," she said, drawing out the jars. Ida noted the look of desire in both their eyes.

"We are grateful," Mr. Coble returned. "There is so little available to us in the city. We live more hour-to-hour than day-by-day, although it has been getting somewhat better."

"I have sausage as well, Mr. Coble," Ida returned, pleased to pull out two large rings.

"An extravagant gesture," Mr. Coble said with teary eyes. "Please, call me Rudolf."

Dinner had been eaten, the satisfied look of slightly filled stomachs obvious on the faces of Ida's hosts. Several hours later, she curled up on a straw-filled mattress in the corner of the shelter, thinking of her days in the camps. The only difference tonight was the absence of severe hunger, abusive guards, and hundreds of other women's bodies.

The next morning Ida made an excuse to her hosts of her plans to spend the day at the relief agency seeking information on her aunt and uncle, assuring them that she had a knife for protection. Ida hoped this would dissipate Mrs. Sonntag's need to accompany her for protection. The ruse worked, or, so she thought at the time. She set out for the meeting place in a prearranged destination in the city conveyed by a craftily applied code known to the sisters. Most were already there, using the password to gain entry.

The meeting place was in a partially bombed-out church still serving its struggling and starving members, in an out-of-the way root cellar. The gathering was scheduled to last less than an hour to minimize the chance of discovery. All made a showing of their arms, vacant of tattooed numbers from the camps, a prerequisite for attending. A record was kept: names, current addresses, tattooed numbers, and targets. Code names and passwords were devised, each signifying the delivery to intended targets, of which there were forty. They would increase to include others as time went on.

Another gathering was scheduled two months in the future in a different Berlin location. Each sister was given an assignment and goal. Failure was not an opinion. Success would separate the talkers from the doers. Ida learned, however, that the secret meeting had been observed.

A smile crossed the face of the observer. Yes, this would do. An immediate need had arisen. This group would serve nicely. Another plot, unknown to the sisters, was already in play. It would prove to be an uncanny alliance, its secrecy lasting years.

CHAPTER THIRTEEN

Present Day – South Carolina

Ken, with Gavin's permission, traced the package sent to his friend. Indeed, it was sent from Greenville, South Carolina. Upon further investigation, the package, with a return address only and no name, was sent from the home of a *David Schmidt*. Ken acquired a phone number and presented it to Gavin less than a week after their return from Washington, D.C.

Gavin looked at the phone number. "I suppose I should call," was all he said. Gavin looked weary. Ken suspected the situation was getting to him.

"Give yourself a day or two."

Gavin looked up. "You know, there was a day I was enthralled by the hunt. Not anymore. Nowadays, I just want peace."

Ken, sensitive to Gavin's age, placed his hand on Gavin's shoulder. "I understand completely. Peace is a coveted prize. On the other hand, you may just find reasons for jubilation."

"You have suggested as much on a previous occasion," Gavin returned. "I remain hopeful."

Several days later, Gavin made the phone call. He didn't share with Carole his intent, a decided departure for him. He was nervous as he made the call, sleeping little the night before, conjuring up the "what-ifs" in his mind all through the night.

On the third ring, a voice answered.

"Hello."

"I am looking for a David Schmidt. My name is Gavin Tandermann from the Myrtle Beach area. I recently received a package from your address. I understand it was sent from my deceased sister, Ida Tandermann Schmidt."

"Oh my! That would be my mother. It was her request to send it soon after her death, but we had no idea who the receiving party was. We just had a name and address. Did I hear you say she was your sister?" the voice on the other end asked.

"Her letter indicates I am."

"I don't understand."

Gavin composed himself before responding. "Until the package arrived, I had no idea I had a sister."

"I see."

Gavin cocked his head in mild confusion before replying. "Do you?"

There was some hesitation before David Schmidt spoke again. "My mother was very adamant the package be sent after her death. When I asked who Gavin Tandermann was, she simply replied, 'Someone from my former days.' We had no idea she had a brother. She never spoke of her past."

"Well, Mr. Schmidt, according to her letter, she had *two* brothers. There was a younger brother, Carl, who is now also deceased."

"Are you saying you didn't know of your brother's existence either?"

"I had no idea I had a sister and a brother until the package arrived."

There was a slight pause before David spoke again. "I can't imagine why anyone would keep such a secret."

"I wish I knew; which brings me to this phone call. I am hoping for answers. I thought you might be of help."

David offered a thought. "Mr. Tandermann, I will help in any way I can. I, too, have questions. It would appear you are my uncle, and that delights me. I would very much like to meet you. I have uncles and aunts on my father's side, but none I knew of, until now, on my mother's side. Would you consider a visit to Greenville so we could meet and get to know each other? My wife is a great cook. We will introduce you to our children, three boys and a girl, great-nieces and nephews you, apparently, also never knew you had until now."

Gavin was taken back by the generous offer, nearly overwhelmed by the thought of meeting blood relatives. "Are you sure?"

"Of course! It appears we have much to discuss and discover. The fact my mother wanted the package sent without informing us of its contents or who it was sent to has been bothering me more than I care to admit. I would be grateful for your thoughts."

"Then I will bring the contents of the package with me for you to see. Did my sister live with you?" Gavin asked with a hint of hesitation.

"No. She lived next door, so we were able to keep an eye on her. My wife did most of the checking in. They got along famously. I swear, I felt in the way at times."

"I'm pleased she had family to support her."

"Are you married, sir?" David asked respectfully.

"Yes, and happily so for nearly thirty years. My dear wife, Carole, will be ecstatic when I tell her about your invitation."

"Then please, let's set a date."

Less than a month later, Gavin and Carole pulled into the driveway of David and Corrine Schmidt's house in Greenville, South Carolina. The couple was awaiting their arrival in the front yard since Gavin had called from the road to verify the last of directions to their home.

The couples greeted each other warmly. Carole stepped back in complete awe. "My goodness, Gavin! David is a younger version of you! The resemblance is uncanny," she said, scanning back and forth between the older and the younger. She then pulled a photo from her wallet of Gavin in his younger days.

"You're right!" Corrine Schmidt said readily, looking at the photo. "What a trip!"

"Now I know where I got my good looks," David said jovially. "I look nothing like my father. At one point, I wondered whether my mom had a secret."

"Apparently the only secret she had was that she had two brothers she never talked about," Carole quipped.

Corrine nodded. "A mystery, for sure. I must confess I feel a bit slighted. I thought Ida and I were close. To keep such a secret, it must have been important to her."

It was almost as though Carole had reunited with a life-long friend. Corrine was just as outgoing and wide open as Carole. The two women hit it off immediately. Gavin smiled, knowing his wife was in her element. As if the four had known each other for years, the conversation flowed among them with hardly a pause.

After dinner, they turned to examining and discussing the items Gavin brought from the package he'd received. Gavin shared with the Schmidt's their experience visiting the Holocaust Museum in Washington, D.C. and the recommendations from Kathe Hohman, the German translator.

"So, if I understand what you're saying, you intend to determine whether you and your brother where part of the Kindertransport effort," David summarized, "and when your parents expected your return."

"Yes, I suppose," Gavin replied. "This may explain why my British family never adopted me. They were hoping for the return of my biological parents."

"Perhaps. That would be something I'd be willing to research for you, Uncle Gavin, if you'd like my help," David offered. "This whole affair is taking on a life of its own. If my mother knew you and her other brother…"

"Carl," Gavin supplied.

"Yes, Carl. If she knew you were both taken away for your safety, and didn't come forward all these years to reestablish her relationship, there must have been a very good reason. It will eat me alive until I know what motivated her to keep such a secret."

Gavin considered what David shared. "Then you would be interested in doing the research? We were told our questions might be answered by the World Jewish Relief Organization. Would you be willing to contact them, David?"

"I would relish the opportunity."

"Then by all means, proceed with my blessing," Gavin replied with a thoughtful look. "I want to know her; my sister. What was she like?"

David smiled. "She was a beautiful person, both inside and out. Don't get me wrong, I loved my father as well, but my mother, well, she was wily and astute. I can only describe her as one who must have lived many lifetimes. She seemed to revel in us as a family, as though our very presence was a special gift. She never failed to let us know how much we meant to her. Not a day would go by that she would not remind us of what a blessing we were to her. We always felt special." He paused, then added, "There was another side, however, and it could be frightening."

"What do you mean?" Carole asked.

"The first time I saw it was when I was being bullied by a kid in the neighborhood. It had been happening for some time, but I kept it to myself. One day, my mother witnessed the kid pushing me to the ground. The next thing I knew, my mother had the kid against the house two feet from the ground. What I remember most was the depth of her rage. I almost didn't recognize her. I was more afraid of her at that moment then I was of the bully. Then my father arrived home from work and came to the kid's rescue. It took a bit of effort to get my mother to release the guy. It was as if she had been transported somewhere else."

"Did this happen often?" Carole probed.

"I wouldn't say *often,* but it was memorable when it did occur. There was this one time when our oldest son was to be benched for three games by his soccer coach for being late to one practice. My mother listened to our son's recital of the punishment. The same look came across her face, the look she had when I was bullied by the neighbor's son. Her hands were balled into fists. She said nothing, and simply left the room. The next day my son came home from soccer practice announcing the coach amended his punishment to being benched for just one game instead of three. My mother never commented but was smiling the rest of the evening. The next time I saw the soccer coach, who was a jerk most of the time, he couldn't have been more sportsmanlike to the team. I think my mother got to him, someway, somehow. The kids actually ended up with a winning season. When I commented to her later that the coach had conducted himself as a gentleman for the rest of the season, she said simply, "Sometimes a persuasive gesture can have lasting effects."

"What did she mean?" Gavin asked.

"I never found out. When I asked her what she meant, she didn't comment. Say, I had a thought. My children and their families are coming over tomorrow afternoon for lunch to meet you. We would have time in the morning to visit my parents' graves, if you'd like. We have the time."

"Oh. Why, of course," Gavin replied, moved by the suggestion.

The next morning David picked up Gavin and Carole at their motel, while Corrine stayed behind to prepare lunch. The Jewish cemetery turned out to be located at the end of the road in David's small community.

"This is a bit surreal," Gavin commented when David pointed to his parents' gravesite. Ida Tandermann Schmidt was buried beside her husband, Jacob David Schmidt. "Just weeks ago I didn't know she existed. Now, here I am standing at her grave."

"It looks like Aunt Helen was here, either late yesterday, or early this morning. The flowers are still fresh," David commented.

"Aunt Helen?" Carole inquired.

"My mother's best friend. Her proper name is Helena Ilg. We've always called her 'Aunt Helen.' She'll be joining us for lunch this afternoon. My mother was very specific with me and my sister that after her passing we were to look after Aunt Helen. And we do. My parents lived next door to us, and Aunt Helen lives in a small bungalow just across the street after years of living with us."

"You grew up with her in the house?" Gavin asked.

"Yes, for the most part. She was always around, helping out with us kids. She worked at the local library as long as I can remember. She bought one of the homes down the street. It was paid for entirely in cash."

"My, that was some saving effort. And your parents' home, David? What is to become of it?"

"Oh. My mother willed it to Aunt Helen with all expenses being paid by my mother's estate. Not that the estate is large to my knowledge, but enough to cover the costs. Upon Aunt Helen's death, the property will pass to me and my sister, Thea. Aunt Helen is in the process of selling her place."

"How generous of your mother," Gavin commented. "Your Aunt Helen is very fortunate to have such a good friend."

"I agree. Then again, Aunt Helen has always been very good to us."

CHAPTER FOURTEEN

"An immoral society betrays humanity because it
betrays the basis for humanity, which is memory.
A moral society is commited to memory."

Elie Wiesel, 1995

Berlin – January 1946

The winter of 1945 set upon Germany with a vengeance. Even so, the sisters met. For this occasion, it was a different location in Berlin, with staggered visits for the protection of all. The encounters were emotional and revealing, each presenting her individual progress to date. It proved to be impressive. The goal was being achieved with the utmost attention to detail, as prescribed.

There were readings through this day, a reminder of why the sisters deployed their enormous strength in response to the Nazi regime's hideous demonstration of debased humanity. The readings would continue each time the sisters met, now in groups of five. Memory. It is always about memory. This was an integral part of each meeting.

"They could have taken anything away from me, but not my little comb. I combed my hair every day. You could find red traces from the never-ending lice. No ointment was given. You couldn't go and see a doctor for lice. The only recourse was to scratch incessantly. After a time, some stopped scratching and gave up and sat in the corner, waiting to die. In time their bodies were carried away to the ovens." (062506)

"The stove. An opportunity to heat something. An impossibility to do this for one hundred women with one hundred fifty children. One stove in the day room, one in the washroom, electric burners for large pans with children's food, for baby food, for wash water, for toasting bread, or drying diapers. The child is often weakened after three-to-ten weeks of sickness and needs extra food. There was none." (012052)

"In the yard beside the building, the women were given a small towel and a piece of soap and taken into the left side of the building, where they had to undress. They were told they had to wash well, as this was important in the camp where they were going. In the gas chamber, the SS shouted to them: 'Wash well, there's no hurry.' The dead bodies were taken out of the gas chamber by dragging them with hooks." (050858)

Midday, the readings were suddenly interrupted by two female intruders. The sisters, alarmed they were discovered, sought to protect themselves, drawing from beneath their garments knives and guns.

"There is no need for violence," one intruder announced. "There has been enough already. We come in peace."

Ida was dumbfounded. "Mrs. Sonntag! What are you doing here? It is not safe for you."

"Nor for you, child, I assure you. I am not here to judge."

The sisters murmured among themselves. They were not about to tolerate an intrusion. Ida was quick to speak before the matter got out of hand. "You must explain yourself, Mrs. Sonntag, immediately!"

"I, and my sister," Sarah Sonntag began, gesturing toward the woman beside her, "are aware of your plan. There is no intent on our part to reveal your undertakings, I can assure you."

"What makes you think you will leave here alive?" one of the sisters spat. The others nodded their agreement, murmuring angrily among themselves.

"I also bear a secret which I will entrust to you. So you see, we will exchange secret-for-secret, and we will all do what we must do. There is no other way."

Then Sarah Sonntag shared an event with the sisters. They were stunned by the revelation, looking at each other questioningly when she had finished the telling.

"You can't be serious?" Ida said at the end of the prolonged oration, complete with history. "You're asking us to raise a child? Why would we agree to do such a thing? It was your sister who made the decision. Why involve us?"

"There is no other way."

"This is not our responsibility. We have endured enough. You are suggesting years of involvement. How is this possible? We cannot do as you ask, especially given the child's heritage," Ida stated, adamant in her position.

The sisters were quiet, digesting this twist of events with murmured discussion. Finally a voice from the group spoke. "Perhaps we can." They all turned toward the sister who spoke with questioning eyes. "Perhaps we *can* do the right thing," she began. "After all the evil, perhaps if we take on this responsibility, we may be able to look back knowing we did not allow a sickness of the mind and heart to occur this time. We were powerless in the camps. We are not now. This time we have the luxury of choice. I believe I may find such a memory reassuring."

The sisters looked at each other. Ida turned to Sarah Sonntag and her sister. "We must talk among ourselves. You must go now."

The sisters talked. The situation was presented, questions were asked, and a decision was made. All wanted to see the child for themselves. Ida made arrangements for the group to quickly visit the home of Sarah Sonntag's sister to get a glimpse of the child, now nearly five years old. All agreed the child was beautiful.

It was Ida who was most moved by the sight of the child playing quietly on the floor with homemade toys. She remembered the joy of being with her young brothers, still yearning for them. Perhaps taking in this child would ease the feeling of loss.

Ida was the last to leave the home after the others trickled out at staggered times so as not to raise suspicion. She turned to Mrs. Sonntag. "I will take the child," was all she said at first.

Sarah Sonntag was taken aback by the reversal in Ida's demeanor. "I did not expect this from you. How will you explain this to your Ms. Kaiser?"

"I will simply say a child as beautiful as this one should not be without guardians. Ms. Kaiser is a good Christian woman. She will understand and approve. Are there papers? A certificate of birth indicating the child's lineage?"

"There are papers. My sister, Frieda, had the presence of mind to take them."

"Frieda was daring in her actions. If caught, she would have been tortured and put to death. We must have other papers. False papers of identity. Several, perhaps."

"Frieda assures me this has been accomplished prior to her collusion with the child's nanny, who is now dead. Killed by the Russians. Yes. For sure. I already have the false papers. There are ways to accomplish this. There is something else. An identifying mark on the child."

Ida cocked her head questioningly. She watched Sarah as she went to the child and removed the sock from the young one's right foot. On the plantar surface of the big toe was a tattooed symbol. Sarah told Ida what Frieda learned and shared with her about the tattoo.

"How bizarre," Ida commented when Sarah finished her summary. She looked at the older woman more closely. "What can

I expect from you, if I take the child?"

A sly smile crossed Mrs. Sonntag's face. "I will keep your secret and those of the other women. I don't agree with what you are doing, but I understand the motivation and will support you in any way. I cannot, and will not, however, be directly involved. You will have me as a resource, an adviser, and benefactor. That is all I can do."

"It is enough." Ida turned to look at the child still playing. "I have something to do tomorrow."

"As before, when you visited last."

Ida did not comment for a time, surprised at Sarah's intuition and knowing. "I will come for the child in two mornings."

"There is another matter of interest in these affairs." Sarah Sonntag shared another revelation."

Ida eyed her intently before speaking again. "Just so we understand each other, I suspect you of some form of treachery."

"I expected as much." Sarah placed her hand gently on Ida's shoulder. "I have lost family as well. I fear for you, my child. Your anger goes deeper than most. Anger is not the answer. It will destroy you."

Ida turned, her face in a hideous scowl. "For now, anger is all I have. It gives me purpose."

"You are still young, Ida. You can forget."

"That is where you are wrong. It is not about forgetting. It is about memory. Forgetting allows this to happen again. Memory repels. We must remember and remain angry. It was a docile nation that allowed atrocities to occur. It will be an angry nation that shall not allow such action again. Of that I am certain."

Ida returned to the meeting point and informed the sisters of her decision and the other consequences surrounding the child. They all took a vow of secrecy and support. The resolve of the sisters would produce displays of unity for years to come. In the end, they would die with their secrets, satisfied justice was served, and a life saved.

"My father was no longer. He was gassed shortly after arrival at the camp. My mother died in my arms nine months later. A family disintegrated. What had we done to merit such disrespect and disregard? I continued for another two years, watching the watchers wreak havoc and insolence on those of their station. I vowed, that in the end, their plight would be in my hands. They would come to terms with their decision, and remember." (Ida Ann Tandermann -022848)

CHAPTER FIFTEEN

Donna and Ken were having breakfast with the Tandermanns at their favorite restaurant when Gavin's cell phone rang. He looked at the caller ID. It was his newfound nephew, David Schmidt.

"David! Good Morning!" Gavin answered jovially. "I have Carole and our neighbors, Donna and Ken, with me. Can I place them on speaker phone?"

"Good Morning, Uncle Gavin, Aunt Carole, and neighbors. Yes, it's all good."

"You know, I must confess. I like the sound of 'Uncle Gavin'. What have you been up to?"

"I am rather excited. Upon forwarding your certified birth certificate, and that of your brother Carl's to the World Jewish Relief Organization, they have assured me your records have been religiously preserved, along with the names of your father, mother, and sister."

"Ida, your mother."

"Yes."

There was a brief pause in the conversation before Gavin spoke. "Then it's true. Carl and I were sent away to ensure our safety."

"There is no doubt, Uncle. There is one more thing. The relief organization included a copy of a letter from your mother to the two families who took you and your brother in for safety and remained your guardians. There is also information on your sister you should be aware of."

Gavin became teary and couldn't speak. Carole came to his rescue.

"David, is there any chance you can visit with us anytime soon and bring these papers with you? If not, we can always come to Greenville."

"Now that's the thing, Aunt Carole. I may not have shared, but Corrine and I have a condo in Myrtle Beach. We were planning a July 4th weekend on the beach. We've invited Aunt Helen to join us as well as two of our three children and their families. The other set is out of state. Everyone loves to shop the outlets."

Donna seized the moment. "David, this is Donna. Ken and I have a July 4th barbecue at our home every year. Could we coax all of you into joining us while you're here? We'd love to meet you. Gavin and Carole have shared their delight in connecting with you and your family."

"Your offer is so very kind. I will share your invitation with Corrine, Aunt Helen, and the rest. I'm certain most will attend if they don't already have plans. This family loves parties and are not shy about meeting new people."

"Wonderful!" Donna returned enthusiastically.

"Just so you know," Gavin interjected, "we are all neighbors, Ken, Donna, and ourselves. Then there is an extended family just up the road from us that include our three grandchildren. To sweeten the pot, I plan on a brunch for all the next day."

"Your Uncle Gavin is known for miles around for his cooking, especially his desserts. I'd take advantage of this, if I were you, David," Carole interjected.

"My! It sounds like I've been missing out for years. Count us all in, for sure!"

⁂

The weather for Donna and Ken's July 4th barbecue was a "chamber of commerce" day, an expression often used by the tourist industry to indicate perfect climate conditions for visitors to their community. The large turnout of friends and family throughout the day and evening was a yearly occurrence, and no less so this year. David, Corrine and their family, along with Aunt Helen, arrived mid-afternoon and immediately felt at home, joining in the festivities.

Gavin introduced the Schmidt family and Aunt Helen to Megan, Greg, and little Ken Bishop, Ken's daughter, son-in-law, and grandson. Lacy Sue and Saul Larson and their three children, the older sister Mary, and the younger twins, Gavin and Carole were introduced as Gavin's family as well.

Donna was watching Gavin's newfound family members from her hostess position, weaving about among the guests to make sure everyone was comfortable and had their drinks. David, in her opinion, was a look-alike of Gavin, and just as warm and inviting as his uncle. Corrine was an outburst of laughter and playfulness, much the same as Carole. Aunt Helen, to Donna, was a beautiful, older woman with an almost regal self-possessed poise bespeaking unmistakable character.

"My, your friends know how to welcome newcomers," Corrine said to Carole after numerous introductions through the day.

"This is make-yourself-at-home country," Carole returned. "What did all of you do this morning?"

Just then Aunt Helen joined the conversation. "Oh," Aunt Helen answered. "We walked the beach and the kids fed the seagulls.

It was a beautiful start to the day. We were on the beach at sunrise. It was breathtaking!"

"David sat on the beach most of the morning reading his current Kindle download, *Guardian of the Damned*. He is so excited to be here, Carole. Connecting with his uncle has been the event of the year," Corrine shared.

"Gavin feels the same way. This whole affair has been both unnerving and adventurous at the same time. The addition of newfound family is especially exciting."

Donna and Ken, ever the patriots, each gave a short speech and read a poem invoking the day's recognition of independence and freedom. A toast was met by clinking glasses, applause, and the waving of mini-flags.

Donna, standing near Aunt Helen after the toast, observed she seemed suddenly unsteady. Rushing to her aid, Donna assisted the older woman with an arm of support.

"What's wrong, Aunt Helen?"

"Oh my. I think I've had too much sun today," the older woman replied, while attempting to balance herself. David and Corrine immediately came forward in concern.

"Perhaps a short rest in the guest room would be in order," Donna offered. Lacy Sue, given her nursing experience, took blood pressure readings.

"Yes, Aunt Helen. It can't hurt. Let's get you a glass of water as well. Perhaps you are a bit dehydrated," Corrine offered and immediately went to secure one.

Donna, Ken, David, and Corrine navigated Aunt Helen into the house. After she drank some water, she allowed her shoes to be removed and be positioned on the bed for a brief rest. A pillow and light blanket completed the ministry.

"I'm embarrassed by all the fuss," Aunt Helen shared in an almost exhausted tone.

"No need to be," Donna replied softly after Lacy Sue took the older woman's blood pressure once again. "Rest for now. I'll check on you in a few minutes."

True to her word, every fifteen minutes Donna entered the house to check on Aunt Helen, giving a report each time to David, Corrine, and Lacy Sue.

"She's snoring like a baby!" Donna announced after the second check. "She has even kicked the covers off. I think she is okay. Her color is good and her breathing is even."

"She'd be embarrassed to know she snores. Aunt Helen is such a lady!" David announced conspiratorially.

"She will never know from me," Donna returned.

Forty-five minutes later, Aunt Helen made her way to Donna and Ken's patio. David and Corrine immediately went to her.

"Feeling better?" David asked.

"Much!" was the crisp reply from Aunt Helen. "There's nothing like a good catnap."

That, thought Corrine, was Aunt Helen. Strong, stalwart, and resolute. A "never-let-'em-see-you-sweat" kinda gal.

The evening waned toward quiet conversation, as guests took their leave, thanking Donna and Ken for their hospitality.

"I think that's it for us, as well," David announced to indicate their departure for the evening. "I'm told the morning will realize a fabulous brunch, though."

"Indeed!" Gavin returned. "Do you see that home with the blue shutters?" he asked, pointing a finger across the country road. "That's our place. Just to the right, down the path, is the home of Lacy Sue and Saul Larson, and our grandchildren."

"My! I hadn't realized you all live so close to each other."

"It's by design, I can assure you. I suggest you follow today's driving directions to find our home tomorrow. Ken and Donna and the Larsons will all be joining us."

"Sounds like more fun," David said as he ushered Aunt Helen and the rest of the family into the backseat of the vehicle.

"Oh," Carole interjected. "Bring an appetite. Gavin is known far and wide for his culinary skills."

※

The next morning the vehicle carrying David, Corrine, Aunt Helen, and the rest of the family, pulled into Gavin and Carole's driveway. They were greeted by the Larson twins and their older sister, Mary. Mary was maneuvering a drone. The twins were in rapt attention.

"Hi!" little Carole said to the folks exiting their vehicle. "You were here yesterday."

"Yes, we were," Corrine replied, delighted by the children. "We had such a good time, we decided to return today. Is that okay?"

"Oh, sure," replied little Gavin. "We like Grandpa's friends."

"We like Grandpa's grandchildren," Corrine returned cheerfully, fully captivated with the three of them.

"I'll let them know you are here," Mary offered, maneuvering the drone for a smooth landing.

"No need, Mary. I saw them pull up, but thanks, sweetie," Grandpa Gavin said, coming down the driveway from the back of the house with Carole. "Let your mom and dad know our guests have arrived though, would you, honey? We should be eating shortly."

"I'll text them," Mary returned.

"A drone, huh?" David commented, while opening the back door of the vehicle to assist the family's exit.

"Our grandchildren are into the drone thing these days. Mary is especially technical in all things that are computer-related, but has taken a special interest in drone technology. How this dovetails into studies in psychology is another question for her grandparents. We admit we retain a deficit in current technology trends."

"It's not only a deficit, it's a clear inability to 'get it'," Carole added. "In our day, it was the telephone. Along came the cell phone. I've learned to live with that and the texting thing. Our grandkids don't talk to us unless we text them! It doesn't stop there. Now there's social media. Facebook, Twitter, LinkedIn, Google, YouTube, Instagram, Pinterest, Tumble, Snapchat, Vine, blogging, and logging. Whatever happened to just picking up the telephone to talk? Does anyone write a thank-you note anymore? Or forward a letter? I feel so out of it."

"My mother would often say the same thing," David admitted. "She didn't understand the advances in technology. Several years back, I bought her a simple computer and spent hours teaching her how to use it. She finally gave up in frustration. She said she felt out of her league."

"That's it! That's exactly how I feel! Out of my league," Carole admitted.

Corrine smiled knowingly. "We're younger than you and yet we struggle as well. Our children and grandchildren have come to call us 'Pilgrims' because of our lack of technological expertise. My younger sister died in 1998 of cancer. If she were to come back today, she wouldn't understand a word of our current lingo. There's a whole generation or two of us who struggle to keep up."

"I'm glad to know I'm not alone," Carole quipped.

Gavin and Carole ushered David, Corrine, Aunt Helen, and the rest of the family toward the back of the house. There on the patio, with a display of Southern elegance, was a mid-morning offering of coffee and Gavin-baked pastries.

"Oh my goodness," Corrine cooed. "Gavin, is this you're doing?"

"It is, indeed," Carole returned. "I warned you your Uncle Gavin is a master at baking and cooking."

"Please help yourself. Brunch will be ready in a little while," Gavin offered. Within moments, the Larson family appeared, all five of them.

"Grandpa! You made our favorites!" little Gavin Larson acknowledged gratefully.

"Nothing is too good for our 'kids'," Gavin replied, a smiled laced across his face.

"Grandpa, you are a gem!" little Carole said with love in her voice. "Our one and only Grandpa and Grandma for sure!"

The Tandermanns' eyes grew teary. Their grandchildren were the best of life. In that they had no doubt.

Lacy Sue and Saul exchanged greetings with their guests after Lacy Sue placed a large bowl of fresh berry salad on the patio sideboard; a blend of strawberries, raspberries, blueberries, and blackberries, with a touch of sugar.

"We are about ready," Carole announced, helping Gavin and Saul carry dishes out to the sideboard. "Get it while it's hot!"

The kids were served first, with the adults following. Everyone was enjoying the sumptuous brunch of endless choices in between conversation related to current events and personal experiences. The children, having finished eating, wanted Mary to continue flying the drone in the front yard. Mary agreed.

"I'm taking the kids to the front yard for more drone time," Mary announced to her parents.

"Would it be all right if I joined you? I've never seen one fly before today," Aunt Helen asked.

"Sure. We'll show you how it works," young Gavin said, taking Aunt Helen's hand to escort her to the front of the house. Mary grabbed a folding chair for Aunt Helen to sit on while she watched.

The rest of the family followed, leaving Gavin, Carole, David, Corrine, Lacy Sue, and Saul sitting together at one of the tables.

"The children are charming," Corrine observed, her face laced in a smile as she watched them take their leave. Lacy Sue and Saul acknowledged Corrine's complement.

"They can be challenging at times, but worth it!" Lacy Sue returned.

"Fortunately, we have reinforcements," Saul added, nodding toward the children's grandparents.

"Speaking of grandparents," David began, "perhaps this is the perfect time to go over the information forwarded to me by the World Jewish Relief Organization."

"Yes, by all means," Gavin said.

"As I mentioned in our last telephone conversation, a copy of a letter from your mother, my grandmother, Hinkle Tandermann, was forwarded by the office of the Kindertransport effort to each of the two British families who became guardians for you and your brother. I can either read them aloud for the benefit of all, or you can read it privately, Uncle Gavin, and share its contents when you are ready."

Gavin hesitated before making his decision. "Everyone here is family and close friends who have supported me in my quest to understand my sister's decision. So, please read it aloud so all can hear."

"Of course. By the way, the original was written in German, but the World Jewish Relief Organization was kind enough to translate it into English. I have both the German and the English versions for your file, Uncle Gavin."

David took out the letter from a folder he had placed to the side and began to read.

Dear British Family: No words can adequately convey our gratitude for your kind gesture to serve as guardians for our son until such time

we are able to unite with him again. Circumstance beyond our contro,
of which you are aware, have forced us to surrender him to your loving
care. Our indebtedness to you knows no bounds.
Until we can thank you in person, we remain
Respectfully Yours,
Hinkle Tandermann – September 1, 1939

"So your mother and father had every intention of coming back for you and your brother, Gavin," Carole confirmed.

"Yes," Gavin returned somberly. "This letter also confirms my guardians knew of their intent to return as well. What of my sister, though?"

"Apparently, the British family who would have taken your sister backed out of the arrangement at the last minute due to an extended health emergency. Due to a clerical error, this was not conveyed until you and your family were already at the train station. There was every intention of finding another family to take your sister in, but very little time to do so. Unfortunately, the borders were closed shortly thereafter."

"David, does the World Jewish Relief Organization have any follow-up records indicating what became of parents who did not return for their children?" Donna asked.

"I inquired, but only relatives claiming the children on behalf of deceased parents are on record."

"Would they still have a record of the name of the other family who took in Carl?" Lacy Sue questioned.

"I almost asked, but concluded they must be dead by now and such information would be of little use," David explained.

"Not necessarily," Donna jumped in. "We know that both sets of guardians are deceased, but it may be worth exploring whether family or friends of the two British families have any knowledge of the time and the circumstances. I would be willing to explore this possibility. All I would need is the name and address of the guardians to begin a search."

"I think it is worth following up every last detail just to be sure every aspect of this situation has been accounted for," Lacy Sue concurred.

"Then I will inquire and see if or when I can have the information forwarded. There is still the question of whether Carl married and had children. If so, they would be my aunt and cousins and nieces and nephews to you, Uncle Gavin. I'd like to explore this possibility. Would that be agreeable to you?" David queried his uncle.

"My, this is building momentum. Yes, to all of your offers to assist."

CHAPTER SIXTEEN

"Because I remember, I despair. Because I
remember, I have the duty to reject despair. I
remember the killers, I remember the victims,
even as I struggle to invent a thousand and
one reasons to hope."

Elie Wiesel, "Hope, Despair, and Memory," 1986

February 1946 – The Netherlands

I da's return, with the child, was met by a shocked Ilse Kaiser.
"What is this? Where did this youngster come from?" Ilse asked
with irritation as Ida entered the home with the toddler in hand.

"The child has no family. I couldn't just ignore the situation,"
Ida struggled to explain.

"You intend to take in a child to live with us?" Ms. Kaiser asked
in disbelief.

"There is no other place," Ida returned with a confidence she
did not feel. Then she thought of reasoning Ms. Kaiser might just
accept. "I look at this child and see the possibility of my return to
God."

Ms. Kaiser looked long and hard at Ida who was maturing at
a rate far beyond her years. While the young woman worked hard
and was respectful, Ms. Kaiser somehow doubted her honesty in this
matter. Her eyes conveyed a resolve behind her action. Two trips to
Berlin, though explained as searches for relatives, seemed unusual,

and she had returned with a young child whose origin she could not or would not explain. Ever the Christian, however, and having had her faith tested severely in the camps, Ms. Kaiser turned her doubts over to a higher power. Even now, her faith would sustain her.

"I was delivered from the camps. You were delivered from the camps. Perhaps God is asking us to deliver this child from the streets," Ms. Kaiser said after a time.

"Yes, I am sure it is God's plan," Ida said, feigning a faith she had rejected long ago in a hasty attempt to appease her benefactor.

Winter held the country in a gripping cycle of cold. When they ventured out, they were often met by howling, frigid winds. Thankfully, Ida prepared through the summer and fall for an abundance of wood so they could keep the fire stoked. Again, the third floor presented the best place to protect their bounty against a harsh winter and certain theft. Rumors circulated that some died, ill prepared for the consistent low temperatures, unlike recent winters. Some deaths would not be discovered until early spring, after the snows abated enough to inquire about relatives or friends.

Thankfully, the child provided a distraction from the unrelenting winter chill and indoor doldrums. Ilse Kaiser took to creating fun activities, even relishing her playtime with the young child. Ida could hear them laughing playfully through the activities Ms. Kaiser created for the young one. She told stories, made toys, baked cookies, and built structures from blocks and then they both would knock them to the floor in glee. It was a whole different Ms. Kaiser, who hadn't before known the joy of children, having never married.

Their watch business was slow through the winter, but the little bell atop their front door rang often for those seeking canned and baked goods. One afternoon, as Ida lay with the child for a nap, the front door sounded the bell, indicating someone had entered the shop. Ida could hear Ms. Kaiser bustle to the front from the back room. Her greeting was nondescript, her voice somewhat sharp, though Ida could not make out the conversation.

Arising from the bed, Ida positioned herself for a closer look at the encounter taking place in the watchmaker's front room. Ms. Kaiser was clearly agitated, a scowl replacing her usual buoyant smile for customers.

"You have your nerve coming here," Ms. Kaiser addressed the woman on the other side of the counter. The woman was about the same age as Ms. Kaiser, but wretchedly clothed and under-dressed for such bitter temperatures.

Ida inched forward as the other woman spoke. Something was afoot. Ms. Kaiser was clearly unwelcoming. "I am without firewood for my stove, and I have no food. My Solomon died a year ago, and I have had no support since then. I am without money and am starving. Please, Ida. You must forgive me. My Solomon was the traitor. He was fearful. Surely you can understand!"

"I understand treachery and weakness! Your treachery and weakness doomed my father and sister! It is by the grace of God I survived, and now you come to me seeking forgiveness? How dare you! Tell me, have you forgiven yourself for not having warned us?"

The woman shriveled in a shameful stance, never taking her eyes from Ilse's. "We were best friends, Ilse. We grew up together, along with your sister, Ella. We three played in the streets, went to school together. We shared secrets, and laughed at each other's mistakes, and celebrated our successes. We have history, Ilse. Surely you can understand. Weakness and fear drove us to do what we did. Please! You must forgive me. I have nowhere to turn."

Ida watched and listened intently from her vantage point behind the wall. She could see the two women clearly. It was a long time before Ilse Kaiser could speak, and when she did her voice was dripping with contempt, the words harsh.

"You ask for bread from someone you betrayed. The death of my father and sister are the sum total of your weakness and fear, Dagfried. My family is irreplaceable, and yet you threw them to the wind as if they were nothing. How many others did you betray in support of your weakness and fear, Dagfried? Do you sleep soundly at night? Are you racked in the wee hours of the morning by guilt and remorse? Can you still look at yourself in a mirror without turning away in disgust?"

Ms. Kaiser turned from the woman and roughly grabbed a loaf of bread from the display counter, slamming it on the countertop. "Take it! Leave here and never come back! May every bite serve as a reminder of your loathsome act of treachery!"

Dagfried snatched up the bread, holding it protectively against her chest while taking a bite even before leaving the shop, never looking back or uttering a word of thanks. Ms. Kaiser sat down on the stool behind the counter with bowed head, clearly shaken from the encounter. Ida almost went to her, but thought better of it. She turned away to lie back down beside the child, giving the older woman her privacy.

❧

The days hunkered inside allowed Ida time to reconfigure the third-floor garden and its plantings. She studied the placement of plants and their compatibility with each other, thus encouraging a better yield. After spending hours rebuilding the seedling areas, she carefully placed companion plants in their own areas, separating incompatible plants.

"I don't understand why you are rearranging everything, Ida. It seemed to work well the way it was," Ms. Kaiser commented one day early in the project.

"I am hoping for a bigger yield this year. We are running out of canned goods to sell. I would like our supply to last until the next harvest. For instance, I have cabbage seedlings next to beets, onions, and spinach. I want to avoid placing the cabbage seedlings next to the strawberries and tomatoes. They are incompatible with cabbage."

"I didn't know," Ms. Kaiser returned.

Taking Ms. Kaiser's hand, eager to share, Ida continued in her lesson, leading the older woman to a table on the far end of the room. "Here I have planted corn next to potatoes, peas, squash, and beans. I avoid planting tomatoes close to these. The tomato plants will inhibit the growth of these vegetables.

"I have, instead, paired tomato and basil over here," Ida said, pointing toward another section of the room. "They thrive when planted together. Lettuce loves being near tomatoes, as well as chives or garlic."

"I have planted radishes and carrots together because radishes won't compete for the nutrients needed for the carrots."

Ms. Kaiser looked at the young woman, amazed at her knowledge on the subject. "How did you come to know of such things?"

"My mother. While we had a hired gardener, I would often listen to the two discussing the placement of the plants and I remembered that."

"Where will we get the extra jars we need for canning?"

"We can give a discount to those returning their old jars. It should work."

"You are crafty, Ida. You are a fine business woman."

Ida continued her gardening through the winter, pleased when seedlings and new growth began to appear. Her placement were indeed paying off. She realized she would have to enlarge the garden in the spring and begin creating more storage space as well.

The child brought abundant joy to the two women, along with a sense of purpose and focus. "You did the right thing in bringing the child here, Ida," Ms. Kaiser remarked one day after an especially fun day of play. Ida nodded in agreement, her heart warmed as always by the sight of the little one.

Finally, the spring thaw came and was a welcomed relief. Neighbors were able to venture out to tidy up their properties and visit. Many came into the shop for goods.

Ida was serving customers one afternoon when she noticed Ms. Kaiser in huddled conversation with another neighbor, her face registering shock at whatever information the neighbor was sharing.

Later, during dinner preparations, Ida broached the subject. "You received bad news, Ms. Kaiser? I saw you speaking with Mrs. Wilhelm earlier."

"She told me that Dagfried Soffell is dead."

"Oh. Was she a friend of yours?" Ida asked innocently, remembering the exchange between them only a few months earlier.

"At one time."

"What happened to change that?" Ida continued in her questioning.

"Nothing, child. It is no longer important."

"How did she die?"

Ms. Kaiser fussed around the kitchen, pretending to be involved preparing dinner. Ida knew differently. Finally, her benefactor said, "She had been dead for some time, but no one discovered her body until now. Apparently, a smell coming from her flat caused the authorities to investigate. When they entered, they found her dead. Her body was decomposed, but it was apparent that her throat was slashed."

Ida's hands went up to her face in feigned disbelief. "Oh dear! Who would do such a thing?"

"I am asking myself the same question, Ida."

"Did she have enemies?"

"It would appear she did."

In early May, Ida and the child were outside behind the house next to the chicken coop. It was a beautiful clear day with ideal temperatures. The sky was cloudless. A slight breeze drifted by, bringing benign comfort. Ida was busy preparing a place for additional plantings, while the child played contentedly in the grass. They had recently adopted a very young dog, or the dog had adopted them, appearing at their back door emaciated. The child was instantly smitten, Ida was hesitant, and Ms. Kaiser was wary.

"Does it have fleas?" was the first thing the older woman asked.

"If it does, flea power will take care of it," Ida replied.

"It must belong to someone," Ms. Kaiser suggested.

"Not likely, judging by its condition. It's been abandoned."

"A common occurrence, I suppose."

"Mine," the child announced decidedly.

"Oh, dear. If we return the animal, we will have a major wail on our hands," Ida said, observing the child's budding devotion to the animal.

"Let's bring it in, feed it, bathe it, and wait for it to be claimed," Ms. Kaiser suggested.

That night the dog slept, with a youngster's arm wrapped protectively around him in embrace. Weeks and months passed, with no one laying claim to the handsome animal whom they named Katche. The child and the dog were inseparable. Ida was sure the child was safe with Katche; no bodyguard could have been better. Ida and Ms. Kaiser concluded it was a good decision to keep the dog.

A few weeks later, Ida had a surprise visitor. When the bell at the front door rang, she emerged from the back room to address, who she thought, was a customer. She stopped in her tracks with recognition.

"Sarah Sonntag! What are you doing here? This is highly inappropriate!"

"Yet necessary, I fear," the woman replied weakly. "There is no need to worry about discovery. I watched your Ms. Kaiser leave earlier with the child and the dog for their daily walk."

"You have been spying on us!" came Ida's retort.

"Only to a point. I do no harm, child."

"What reason do you have for intruding on my household?"

Sarah Sonntag did not respond at first, and when she did it was a most unexpected response. "I am dying, Ida. I have a bleed. I grow weaker. I am not a doctor, nor have I been to one, but I suspect I don't have long."

"If this is true, you must surely go to a doctor," Ida insisted.

"For what reason? To prolong a life of unbearable suffering? Germany has a long way to go. The people are suffering; I am just one more. I have business you must take seriously. It must be now. I will not have the strength to return."

Ida shook her head slightly in disbelief, attempting to wrap her mind around this unexpected event of apparent urgency.

"What business, Mrs. Sonntag?"

Sarah Sonntag reached into her pouch and retrieved something. Taking Ida's hand, she transferred the contents. Ida looked down and took an audible inward breath. "These are gold coins!"

"Yes."

"Where do they come from?"

Sarah Sonntag began to share how she came to possess the gold coins. Many of them. After she finished, Ida was unable to speak for a time.

"Are you in danger of discovery?" Ida finally managed to stammer, still trying to make sense of the older woman's story.

"It is doubtful. There is too much confusion, although when the confusion settles, someone will remember."

"What is it you want me to do?" Ida asked, still in shock by the revelation, looking at the coins in her hand.

"I will assist you in the entire transfer. You must protect it for a long time. Make use of it for the child and those with whom you have united in your current efforts."

"The sisters?"

"The *sisters*, as you wish to refer to them. Listen, and listen carefully. The vast majority of our people are wandering the streets in search of food. The German people are still under the control of the Reichsmark, price controls, and rationing, a system doomed to further implode. Our country is operating under a barter system for goods, with little to no confidence in our currency. Our men are dead, my husband and son included, giving us few resources to operate the factories. Workers in the city spend hours each week traveling to outlying areas to exchange their offerings of clothing, jewelry, art-work, even gold teeth to farmers in the hope of food. Then the process begins again the following week. Germany is now under the control of America, Britain, France, and the Soviets. Each entity has imposed its own will. We can't continue this way. I suspect our country will, in time, right itself economically, but until it does, and even *after* it does, what I am entrusting to you will ensure your future if properly managed."

Ida was stunned by Sarah Sonntag's words. "Why?" she returned almost inaudibly.

Sarah stood shrunken, a body shriveled in sickness and defeat. "If only you would permit me to leave a meager legacy, then I could know, in my final hours, that my existence was worth something," she said at first. After a pause and a sigh, she continued, "My Germany is not the Germany I anticipated. We were once strong, proud, and agile. Yes, we endured the undue humiliation after our defeat in the First World War. Perhaps Hitler's way would have delivered us, but it is not to be. He is now dead and Germany is in ruins. I am devastated by the knowledge of the atrocities committed by our leaders. Too many have died. Perhaps, just perhaps, what I do can have lasting benefit for a few of those who have suffered."

Ida said nothing, still processing.

"I must go now. Ms. Kaiser will return soon with the child and the dog." With that announcement, Sarah Sonntag handed Ida an envelope. "Guard this with your life. Do exactly as instructed or suffer the consequences. You will be in Berlin soon? I may be gone by then. If so, remember me. It is all I ask."

Sarah Sonntag turned and left the shop, disappearing into a now-falling heavy rain. Ida would never see her again. It would be years before she understood the extraordinary gesture this woman of strange and forbidding countenance bestowed upon her that day, along with its responsibility.

CHAPTER SEVENTEEN

"It is up to you now, and we shall help you—that
my past does not become your future."

Elie Wiesel, Speech at the UN World Peace Day,
New York, September 21, 2006

Berlin – July 1946

Ms. Kaiser resisted the idea of Ida taking the child with
her on yet another trip to Berlin. "The city is still a
shambles, Ida. It is no place for an innocent," she
protested.

Ida immediately saw the inconsistency in Ms. Kaiser's argument
but responded gently, understanding the woman's growing devotion
to the child. "Berlin is the place where the suffering of the innocent
was conceived, Ms. Kaiser. I wish, however, for the child to revel in
travel. I will make it an adventure for the young mind."

"How long will this continue, Ida? Your search for your aunt
and uncle?"

"Until I am satisfied."

"Your search for family is admirable, Ida. I continue to pray for
you," Ms. Kaiser returned quietly.

The trip was better this time. The rails had improved, and the
connections were not as arduous. The child seemed to enjoy the
adventure, as Ida created stories to keep the youngster engaged along

the way. It wasn't hard to entertain. The child held a natural leaning toward adventure and learning.

Upon their late afternoon arrival in Berlin, Ida headed for Sarah Sonntag's home. She was greeted by Sarah's sister, Frieda, and brother, Rudolf, who communicated the news of Sarah's death the previous week. Ida turned away, surprised by the depth of her sadness at seeing them without their sister.

"My sister gave us explicit instructions, anticipating your arrival," Rudolf Coble continued, after giving Ida a moment to recover her composure.

"Oh?"

Frieda looked down at the child. "Perhaps a cookie?" she asked, smitten by the child.

"Cookie," the child repeated. Frieda took the little one by the hand and walked toward the back of the room delivering the sweet. The child then sat happily, taking cookie in hand.

"You will stay with us tonight, yes?" Rudolf asked Ida. "It will give us time to talk."

"That is very kind. Yes, we will stay. I have brought gifts. More sausage and bread, along with produce from the garden."

"Ah! We will feast first and then talk."

Rudolf and Frieda couldn't have been more accommodating toward Ida and the youngster. The brother and sister were softer-looking versions of the now-deceased Sarah. Before long, the child grew tired. Frieda prepared a straw mattress on the floor and sleep came quickly for young one. Ida noticed how close it was to Frieda's sleeping station. Rudolf began to speak.

"I will forever be indebted to your Ms. Kaiser for her care during my convalescence. If it wasn't for her, I don't think I would be alive today."

Ida nodded. "I understand. I, too, owe her a debt of gratitude I can never repay."

Then Rudolf turned to another subject. "I take heart when I hear stories of rescue, whether it be a rescued body, a rescued soul, or a rescued mind. Each reflects an attempt to recapture our nation's humanity, a humanity I fear we lost along the way. There are days, when I learn more of the atrocities, I am ashamed to be German. We, as a people, will lament these as long as we live."

The room drew quiet for a moment before Rudolf continued. "You are aware of our treasure?" he asked Ida tentatively.

"I am."

"You understand how we came to have possession of it and the utmost need for secrecy?" he probed.

"I fully understand."

Rudolf held out an envelope for Ida. She crossed the room, mindful of his missing leg, and accepted it.

"Read it. Read it entirely, and then ask your questions."

Ida returned to the place on the floor where she was sitting, opened the envelope, and began to read. After reading it again, she looked up at Rudolf and Frieda to summarize her understanding of the instructions.

"I am to set up a dummy corporation, drawing on a Swiss bank account once a year, and only once a year, having the sum wired into the corporation's account. I must anticipate each need for the year before doing so. I must then establish minor business accounts, one to benefit the child and one for each of the sisters. Should a recipient die, that portion shall be distributed evenly to the remaining 'businesses' in addition to their yearly allowance. The sum is staggering!"

"It will have to last the lifetime of the child, and the sisters," was Frieda's reply.

"And you?"

"We have our own Swiss bank account," Rudolf returned.

Ida looked around at their understated surroundings.

Rudolf understood her confusion. "You must never give a hint of your wealth, Ida. You must impress this point upon the beneficiaries. It will only bring questions and investigation. As the German economy improves, and the people move beyond the war, we will enhance our home, but not to the point of obviousness. Bear this in mind, Ida. You and the others must remain in average dwellings, and never show off your wealth. Be mindful, however, none of you should have to work a day in your life, unless you choose to."

"It is money from the Reich, then?" Ida asked innocently.

A sly smile came across Rudolf's face. "A very small portion, I can assure you. You may hear a reference in the future to Hitler's gold. Thousands of bars of gold. Tons of gold. Understand, however, it is other countries' gold Hitler's forces and subordinate gangsters appropriated during their conquests of Poland, Hungry, Austria, Belgium, Romania, as well as the Sudetenland of Czechoslovakia. It is now the people's gold."

"We are *the people*, then?" Ida questioned.

Again, Rudolf's expression took on a look of knowing and focus. "We are an infinitesimal portion of the people ravaged by circumstances beyond our control. So we take an infinitesimal portion of what is rightfully ours. We have earned it through our sufferings and loss, Ida. Remember that. Our sister, Sarah, understood this and was quite insistent we understand our actions before her death. No one is going to pay you for the loss of your family or pay me for the loss of my leg. The suffering of countless people—soldiers, children, mothers, and fathers—cannot be measured in gold, Ida, but we can use our portion to provide some relief to a token number of those suffering. It is up to us, now, to protect it, and its source."

"You served in the German army. Are you not still loyal?"

"I served because not doing so would have meant death. I had to choose between the battlefield and the firing squad. Is all clear? Do you understand, Ida?"

Ida nodded, looking down at the coins in her hand, understanding the measure of freedom they would bring. "Yes, I understand completely. I must go to the sisters." Ida left for the evening, confident the child was cared for and would sleep. She would return in the middle of the night.

The sisters gathered. Each relayed her progress to date. All were satisfied the original outline was being followed, with some deviation when necessary. All-in-all, the plan was intact. They then listened to Ida's depiction of unexpected recent developments, after which some wept in relief, while others prayed in gratitude.

"We must maintain complete secrecy for the rest of our days," Ida reminded them.

The sisters worked out another plan, one that would serve them for years to come.

Returning to the home of Rudolf Coble in the middle of the night, Ida slept several hours before waking at dawn.

"I must leave the child with you," she said to Frieda in the morning. "I will return tomorrow morning and take our leave for home."

"You will be exhausted," was the reply from Sarah Sonntag's sister. "What is so urgent about returning home instead of resting?"

"Ms. Kaiser. I don't wish for her to worry."

"Ah! Ms. Kaiser. A good and gentle soul, my brother tells me. You can rest when you return to her then."

CHAPTER EIGHTEEN

Present Day – South Carolina

Donna's search for the two British families who harbored Gavin and his brother, Carl, through the efforts of the Kindertransport, yielded disappointing results. The trail went cold. Despite her setback, Donna continued, as was her way, researching the whole time period. The books she secured at the gift shop, before departing the Holocaust museum, provided a means, and at the very least, secured in her mind a timeline of events from Hitler's rise to power to Germany's eventual downfall. Examining one of the brochures given her at the book-store, she noticed something especially interesting. She placed a call to David Schmidt.

"Donna! So good to hear from you. Corrine and I are still reminiscing about the gracious hospitality you and Ken afforded us during our recent visit. Aunt Helen is still talking about Uncle Gavin's desserts."

Donna laughed. "I'm so pleased you enjoyed yourselves...*and* the desserts. We so enjoyed having you. I'm calling because I want to share something I came across, something that may prove helpful in a search related to your mother, Ida Ann Tandermann Schmidt. It may help to impact your findings related to your Uncle Gavin's brother, Carl."

"Please. I've done some preliminary overtures toward this end, but would welcome any resources you have."

"I hadn't realized, until today, the United States Holocaust Memorial Museum has a Holocaust Survivors and Victims Resource Center. It assists in discovering the fate of relatives and friends who were victims of persecution during the Nazi era. I was thinking you might do a search of your own to see whether or not anything comes up on your mother. The service is free. You may discover details of her whereabouts after the camps were liberated."

"What a great idea. It certainly can't hurt to try."

"Apparently, after the war, the Allies set up a venue referred to as the International Tracing Service or ITS, to help relatives and families reconnect with each other. Currently held data contains over one hundred million documents related to those victims who experienced arrest, deportation, murder, forced labor, slave labor, and displacement through the end of World War II. There are nearly seventeen and a half million victims related through these documents."

"Wow! I never heard of this."

"I didn't either, until today. Apparently the United States Holocaust Memorial Museum has a full digital copy of the ITS archive, and its available to the public. There's more information of this service on the museum's website."

"I will definitely consider this," David relayed, excitement in his voice. "By the way, I've located Carl's family. As you may remember, he lived in Raleigh, North Carolina. He had three daughters, all living in the area. His wife, Lila, of fifty-nine years, died a year before Carl. I will be contacting the older daughter, Lisa Lebowitz, first, and then invite her to join us for a group phone call."

"Oh, David. She has no idea there is family waiting on the sidelines or aware of the family history, for that matter."

"By all accounts, my communication with her will be a complete surprise. I will keep you advised."

❦

Two Weeks Later –

"Lisa? Are you there?" David asked in a pre-arranged conference call to Lisa Lebowitz, oldest daughter of Carl and Lila Tandermann of Raleigh, North Carolina.

"Yes, I am here, David."

David took the lead. "Perhaps we should all identify ourselves. This is my first time using a conference-call format. I understand at least ten of us have connected thus far. I will go first. My name is David Schmidt. My wife Corrine is on the line as well. I have recently discovered I have an uncle, Gavin Tandermann, and that Carl Tandermann was also my uncle. My mother is Ida Ann Tandermann Schmidt, sister to Gavin and Carl. Would someone else like to introduce themselves?"

There was a brief pause before Gavin spoke. "I am Gavin Tandermann. Recently I learned I had a sister, Ida Tandermann Schmidt, now deceased. This has led to a discovery of nieces and nephews I never knew I had. I thank all of you for being so willing to join us on this conference call. I am sharing my call with my dear wife, Carole, and our daughter, Lacy Sue Larson, along with Ken Daniels and Donna DeShayne, our best friends and neighbors."

"Mr. Tandermann, David, and others. This is Lisa Lebowitz. I am the oldest daughter of Carl and Lila Tandermann. My younger sisters are also on the line, Hannah and Jacqueline. David's initial phone call to us was a complete surprise. We had no idea our father had siblings. He never spoke of any relatives. Now we discover we have other family. My sisters and I are excited by the revelation. What is it that we can help you with?"

Gavin answered, "While my sister lived in Greenville, South Carolina, she knew I lived near Myrtle Beach, South Carolina, and that your father lived in Raleigh, but she never contacted us.

"David tells me he has shared with you the fact that my sister, his mother, was a concentration camp survivor. A letter and parcel she left that David sent to me after she died, according to her instructions, has led us to you, our extended family. I couldn't be more delighted. We are simply looking for any detail, however small, that could shed some light on why she made the decision not to unite with her brothers despite her close proximity."

"This is Hannah. I'm wondering what was in the parcel you received."

"It contained a letter from my sister, a well-worn pouch containing a striped cloth with a star, a metal cup, a spoon, a comb, and a sewing needle. In addition, there were two lists, one a set of numbers and the other a list of names titled *Kapos*. The items in the pouch have been identified as remnants of the camps, but we have no idea how the two lists are related."

"I see," was Hannah's only quiet reply at first. She delivered a surprise no one expected. "I have a parcel as well."

"What do you mean?" Lisa questioned her sister.

"I never said anything, but, a while back, a Priority Mail box arrived, with a portfolio inside. The accompanying letter suggested someone would come along and ask questions. Just about the time it arrived, I had a gall-bladder attack and ended up in the hospital. I put the box on a top shelf in my closet, with the intention of dealing with it once I felt better, but I completely forgot about it until now."

"What's in it?" Lisa asked with a hint of impatience in her voice toward her sister.

"It's in German, so I really can't say. It's pretty old. There are lots of papers, if I remember correctly," came the reply.

Donna had been intently listening and decided to jump into the conversation with a question. "Was the letter signed?"

"I didn't really notice. I know I sound like a space-cadet, but I truly forgot all about it."

Gavin stepped in to rescue his newfound niece. "No harm done. We don't even know whether or not it is related to our search, but if it is in German and old, it may contain a piece of the puzzle as to why my sister chose to keep her existence a secret. I am intrigued."

"I'll dig out the portfolio tonight and send you a copy of the papers in it," Hannah offered.

"Maybe that won't be necessary," Jacqueline, the third sister, said. "Remember our trip?"

"Oh! That's right!" Hannah responded.

Lisa filled her listeners in on their travel plans. "We three sisters spend a week in Myrtle Beach every year. Our reservations are in less than two weeks. We can bring this mysterious portfolio with us and arrange to meet."

David jumped in. "Wonderful! Corrine and I can be there as well. It will give us a chance to get acquainted."

Gavin and Carole smiled at each other before Gavin extended an offer. "David, bring the rest of your family as well. That way everyone can meet each other. We know a great coffee shop with a private room where we can gather when you get to Myrtle Beach. And we'd love to have you all to dinner at our home before you leave the area."

Everyone agreed to the plan and on a sunny morning shortly thereafter, the Tandermann sisters appeared at the Beans Café. Aunt

Helen, though invited, was forced to stay behind due to reoccurring dizzy spells. Corrine had arranged for a neighbor to keep a check on her while they were away. David Schmidt was the first to greet his cousins. There was a strong resemblance between David and his female cousins. "I showed Uncle Gavin the photo you sent of the three of you," he told Lisa. "You could pass as triplets."

"We get that a lot," Jacqueline returned. "Most people just stand there and stare at us, looking from one to the other."

Donna and Ken came forward to meet Gavin's newfound family members. "My! I was told you all looked alike. What are the odds you three, so close in age, would look so much alike? It must be fun!"

"It is," Lisa replied. "We inherited the look-alike gene for sure."

Gavin and Carole emerged from the back room to greet the sisters. "Whoa! So, the photos are true. My brother must have loved perfection because he kept repeating the same look with every daughter," Gavin said proudly.

Gavin and Carole embraced their nieces before ushering them into the private dining room. Lisa carried a small easel, having planned this part of the morning with David. After setting up the easel, she and her sisters displayed old photos of Carl and Lila Tandermann, as well as some taken at their fiftieth wedding anniversary celebration five years ago. David, having suggested the arrangement, contributed to the display with older and more recent photos of his mother and father, Ida Ann Tandermann Schmidt and Jacob Schmidt.

Gavin was overcome by the display. "My sister and brother," was all he said, choked with emotion, the tears running down his face. "How was it I never came to know them?"

Ken placed a reassuring hand on his friend's shoulder. "Don't think about the loss, Gavin. Think about the gain. You have nieces and nephews galore. It's a gift, don't you think?"

Gavin turned to Ken and smiled. "Yes. A gift indeed."

"What surprises me," Donna interjected, "is the resemblance in the family, especially with the women. The Tandermann women look nothing like their mother. Who do you see, Gavin?"

It took a minute for the question to register. Gavin then peered at the photos of his sister, and then looked at the three daughters of Carl and Lila Tandermann. The resemblance among the four was uncanny.

"The girls look like my sister," he said quietly, his face aglow.

"It's as if your sister is here, Gavin," Carole commented. "Add your nephew David to the mix, and you have family. Lots of family."

David walked over to his uncle and hugged him. He then smiled, saying, "I have something for you" and then held out a photo album with pictures of his parents and their children, along with a photo history of Carl and Lila Tandermann and their daughters.

Gavin leafed through the album briefly, appreciating its contents. "Oh. Oh, my goodness," he blurted out as he continued to understand the import of the offering. "I can only say I am speechless."

"For once," Carole retorted with a wink at her husband. The others laughed

"Lacy Sue made the suggestion," David said. "She wanted you to have a permanent reminder of your family."

"Lacy Sue," was all Gavin said. His eyes sparkled with added tears.

Carole invited the family to enjoy the simple breakfast laid out on the buffet. Midway through, Lacy Sue, Saul, and the twins entered the room, having just come from the children's soccer practice. Gavin made a beeline for his adopted family, hugging them all. Carole was not far behind.

"Thank you," Gavin said to Lacy Sue. She hugged him long and hard in understanding.

In the middle of breakfast, Mary Larson entered the room, rushing in to join the occasion after attending an early morning online college lecture. She was introduced to the Tandermann sisters as the oldest of Gavin and Carole's grandchildren before taking a seat next to her brother and sister at a nearby table. After everyone was satisfied by the delicious breakfast, David called the group to order.

"I'm told the portfolio has been laid on the table. Uncle Gavin, Aunt Carole, please be the first to review it. The rest of us will follow with your permission."

Hannah spoke for herself and her sisters. "We decided not to examine the contents until you could, Uncle Gavin. We felt you should be the first."

Carole turned to the ladies. "I don't think I would have had the willpower to bring it without looking at it!"

Lisa, Hannah, and Jacqueline, the daughters of Carl Tandermann laughed, nudging each other playfully. "Well, not all of us were that strong," Lila disclosed, looking at her sister, Jacqueline, conspiratorially.

Jacqueline quickly confessed. "I admit it. I wanted to see what was in it. I'm just naturally curious."

"Nosey is more the word," Hannah quipped.

Everyone smiled at the playfulness among the three women. At the same time, they were impressed the portfolio had not yet been opened. Gavin turned toward the table where it rested. He examined the box it came in before sliding out the contents. On top was a single folder. He opened it, and gasped at what he found.

Carole came forward immediately. "What is it?" she inquired with concern. Gavin didn't say anything initially, but simply stared at the contents. Carole moved closer to get a better look. There was a photo. "Who are they?"

"My mother and father and we three children," Gavin returned, his voice laced with emotion. "It was taken in the spring of 1939, according to the note on the back." He turned to David and the rest of the family to share the photo, allowing it to be passed around.

Additional papers were in the folder. Five were the birth certificates of each family member: Olaf Joseph Tandermann, Hinkle Ruth Helmsely, Ida Ann Tandermann, Gavin Joseph Tandermann, and Carl Robert Tandermann. It was Gavin's family of origin. The sixth paper was the marriage certificate of Olaf and Hinkle Tandermann. The other three papers were in German.

"Someone went to a lot of trouble to document our family beyond question," Gavin said, as he leafed through the enclosures. "But who?"

The room was abuzz as the photo and certificates made their way around before finally being placed on one of the tables for further review. Gavin, in the meantime, examined the other folder in the portfolio, pulling out the sheets of paper it contained. Each sheet was written in German by hand and dated at the top, along with a number beside the date. There were forty sheets in all, the same handwriting on each sheet. Gavin added these to the table, along with the contents of the first parcel.

Donna stepped forward to examine the display, her senses peaked against a background of unearthed, and heretofore, unannounced findings.

CHAPTER NINETEEN

"Our lives no longer belong to use alone; they
belong to all those who need us desperately."

Elie Wiesel, Nobel Peace Prize Acceptance Speech, 1986

The Netherlands – January 1952

Ida, Ilse Kaiser, the child, and Katche, the dog, were functioning well in the seventh year after Germany's downfall. Some would even say they were prospering compared with other families who were still struggling.

There was a larger tale to be told, however. The swaths of ruin across Europe and Asia saw the borders between many nations redrawn. In less than a decade, as a result of Germany and Japan's insane quest for power, four percent of the world's population had been killed. War crime trials leading to executions and prison sentences were the news of the day. The years would realize rising and accumulated tensions, producing a divided Germany and Korea. An eventual Arab-Israeli resolution would continue to be a source of conflict. As Ida observed all of this, it seemed to her that despite the ghastly effects of World War II, governments could not bring about a lasting peace.

The child continued to delight Ida and Ilse in the midst of the ever-changing world events. Ida was insistent on a good education, and secured private tutoring. Ilse argued for public schooling as a more practical way of managing their funds, but Ida seemed to have the necessary funds for the child's education.

At one point, Ms. Kaiser raised the issue. "While I know you are careful with our monies, Ida, still the expense of the child's education exceeds our resource. I can only assume you have another source."

"I didn't tell you?" Ida returned. "How thoughtless of me. My aunt and uncle have kindly offered to sponsor educational expenses. It has been a big relief to know I can count on them for this." This was, of course, not true. Ida could not reveal the true source of her money.

Ilse looked at Ida for a time before responding. "They are doing well in the United States then?"

"Yes. I am grateful the American Red Cross could forward their correspondence to me. Uncle has a good job working for an automaker called Ford and Auntie is working for the school system in a town called Edison, New Jersey."

As providence would have it, word from her aunt and uncle through the American Red Cross was forwarded in the form of a letter to Ida just the year before. At first, her inquiries into their whereabouts were an excuse for sojourns to Berlin to meet with the sisters. Never expecting to find family, they instead, managed to find her. Correspondence between Ida and her aunt and uncle revealed they made the decision to leave Germany in 1942, paying a huge sum of money to be smuggled aboard a merchant vessel headed to the United States. After they arrived, they managed to establish themselves in a German sector of Elizabeth, New Jersey and eventually became U.S. citizens. Hearing of work for her uncle at a nearby automotive assembly plant in Edison prompted their move from Elizabeth to Edison.

"They do not ask you to visit?" Ilse inquired.

"Every letter includes an invitation. I will visit one day."

Ilse questioned the reply. Ida could not tell Ilse that the sisters' work, while near completion, was not yet done. She held concerns about Ilse's health as well. The aging woman had developed a cough. At first it was a simple clearing of the throat, but it had progressed into coughing fits that left her exhausted. At the same time, she was losing weight and tired easily. Ida had taken up much of the work, assisted by the young one where appropriate. Even so, Ida was worried. A visit to the doctor failed to identify the source of the problem.

Within months, Ilse was confined to bed. Ida ensured her comfort by raising the legs of the bed at the head to assist Ilse's breathing, which had become increasingly labored. The days when Ilse ventured to her chair beside the bed to knit had become rare, and soon not at all. The child would venture onto the bed now and then to coax the sick woman to play, but finally gave up when it was obvious Ilse was too weak to play.

From the lack of appetite for food, and long periods of sleep, Ida surmised her friend's end was near. She attended to her every need, determined to be present whenever Ilse awakened. The whole effect was similar to her mother's passing in the camps; weakened and emaciated. The only difference would be in an honorable passing of Ilse, a passing Ida could not provide for her own mother.

One afternoon, Ilse opened her eyes to find Ida sitting beside the bed, holding her hand. "You are of great comfort to me, Ida," the older woman said weakly. "I fear my end is near. The house and the property will be yours. Arrangements have already been made. All will transfer to you upon my death."

Ida was moved beyond expectation. Since her experience in the camps, she had navigated without emotion. Even with the child, she was cautious not to give her heart, or be moved to tears as others might be. Her heart was like a stone. Yet, the imminent passing of this dear, now-shrunken woman, who had harbored her and her parents from the SS only to be taken prisoner herself and lose her family in the effort, was more than Ida could bear. The tears flowed. When there was no one else and no place else to go, Ms. Kaiser provided refuge.

"It is good to see you cry, Ida," the weak voice spoke from the bed. "There is still hope for your heart. Do not be sad, my child. You have given comfort to my soul all these years. And now the little one. Companionship, care, and renewal have been your gifts to me. Yet, you hide a secret, child. That much I know. I pray you find your peace in the future. Thank you, dear one. Remember always that I loved you."

With those words, Ilse Kaiser closed her eyes and, after drawing in a deep and final groaning breath, she died.

Ida sat for some time, still holding the older woman's hand. She was brought back to her final days in Ravensbrück, when she was well enough to leave. She had agonized over where to go. There was no family, and there were no friends. Ms. Kaiser was her only hope. Now it seemed she was once again without family and friends.

Ida sat for a long time, processing the loss of a dear friend and pondering her future. It was almost dark when the child entered the room.

"I am hungry," the youngster said, not grasping the situation.

The announcement jarred Ida from her malaise, reminding her of her responsibilities.

"We shall eat, then," she replied weakly.

Ida ate little, but the child, who was growing by leaps and bounds, ate ravenously. Sleep followed a bath and a bedtime story.

Ida next faced dealing with Ilse's remains. She went across the street to speak with a neighbor. The neighbor understood, and in the middle of the night, Ms. Kaiser's body was removed from the home.

The next morning, while the child was having private lessons, Ms. Kaiser's minister knocked on the door.

"I understand you wish to see me. I am saddened by Mrs. Kaiser's passing and for your loss. How can I be of help?" the minister asked.

Ida was surprised by the quick response from the church. "I wish for cremation rather than burial," Ida announced, much to the surprise of the minister. Ida noted the questioning look on the man's face.

"You understand, of course, cremation is an option so long as it is not in defiance of God. The more normal path would be burial. Was this Ms. Kaiser's wish? She was a faithful Christian. If so, she did not tell me of this arrangement."

Ida had already developed a plan, but did not disclose her intent. Instead she answered respectfully. "I was surprised myself by Ms. Kaiser's deathbed wish. She was very clear, however, and I promised I would carry out her wishes. I think the dying reevaluate their choices toward the end, wouldn't you agree? No doubt you have more experience in these matters than I."

The minister was mollified somewhat by Ida's response. He was powerless to refute her, regardless of his own thoughts. "I will make sure her final wishes are carried out. Would you like a funeral service arranged for Ms. Kaiser?"

"By all means."

Three days later, the church service for Ms. Ilse Kaiser was held. The church was overflowing with neighbors, friends, and supporters. In a quiet moment after the service, Ida Tandermann was presented with the cremated remains of her long-time friend.

She found a quiet corner and wept, holding the urn, the remains of her benefactor, to her heart. It reminded her of another time, a less than holy time, when she let go of her own mother's body, only to see it tossed unceremoniously on a cart headed for an unstated and inhumane end. Perhaps, she concluded, this was her answer to the unanswered. A chance to correct a dehumanizing act with an honorable ceremony.

CHAPTER TWENTY

Present Day – South Carolina

Donna, after the breakfast gathering of the Tandermann sisters, asked Gavin's permission to take photos of each page of the portfolio, along with the items from the first mailing. There was something gnawing at her mind. Such unsettled times often served as markers for discovery, while the details remained elusive, dancing incoherently in the recesses of her mind.

Ken came home the next evening to find his significant other encased in reading. "I know that look," was all he said after a kiss.

"What look?" she asked innocently.

"The look you get when you are involved in an investigation and emotionally pulled in. It's Gavin's situation, isn't it?"

"Ken, don't you think all of this is more than a little bizarre? I can understand why Gavin's mind might be swirling. His sister was either mad or brilliant. I tend to lean toward the latter."

"Why would that be? All we have is a bunch of photographs and objects from the Holocaust. I don't pick up on a deeper message."

"I do. I admit, I don't know why I do, but something is off… *really* off. The second package sent to the Tandermann sisters is especially interesting. I have an appointment tomorrow morning with Herta Cohen to translate the German."

"Whoa! Hold up there! Does Gavin know this?"

"He does. I cleared it with him this afternoon. He's onboard."

"What do you hope to accomplish?"

Donna bowed her head. The question clearly unsettled her. "I don't know, exactly. Perhaps something. Perhaps nothing. I have a feeling. Simply a feeling. That's all I ever go on."

⁂

Donna made a call to her older friend, Herta Cohen. They spoke for some time. Herta understood Donna's questions and invited her to visit to review matters to this point. Two days later, Donna was greeted by Suzanne Seigel.

"Mother has been excited at the prospect of your visit. She so wants to be of help. She's waiting in the sunroom."

Donna entered the sunroom, with Suzanne close behind. She immediately went to Herta to offer an embrace. Donna noted the aging woman's hug was strong, much stronger than on her previous visit, and her color looked good.

"I swear, Herta, you look younger! What have you been doing since I saw you last?" Donna asked jokingly.

"I've been enjoying freedom from the past," was all the older woman said, with a broad smile.

"Then you will have to bottle your freedom and make it available for sale. It will be a best seller, by the looks of you," Donna quipped.

"I just might do that. Now, what do you have to show me?"

Donna placed the five birth certificates and marriage certificate on the coffee table for Herta to examine. She then placed the photos on the table along with the portfolio of copied pages.

Herta took her time, careful in her review. She seemed disturbed as she reviewed the copied pages.

"Is something wrong?" Donna finally asked.

"These pages are personnel records of some of the SS and kapos from Ravensbrück. There are even two *blockführrerinnen*—block overseers—included. These SS were especially feared. Some were accompanied by vicious dogs. I see there is a *rapportführerin*—report overseer—in the mix. These were the ones who handled roll call and general discipline of the prisoners. What I am consumed with is the fact each sheet is complete with former addresses and contact information, along with next of kin. A number has been written at the top of each one. It's apparent the number was added much later, after they were stolen."

"Stolen? How do you know they were stolen?"

Herta looked up at the younger woman. "You would understand if you were a prisoner of the Third Reich. The Nazis were obsessive in their record keeping. It is precisely why we know so much about the Holocaust. They recorded everything. The roll call in the camps, or *appell*, both morning and night, could go on for hours until a proper accounting was assured. It didn't matter the weather or hour of the day. You ate only when the accounting was certified. Mistakes were not tolerated. Every attempt would have been made to destroy records of SS operatives and subordinates when the Red Army and the Allies were near to the camps. A theft would be the only way these records could have survived a chaotic time. Someone was very precise as to what they stole. I find it interesting this folder is confined only to those overseeing the barracks housing Jewish women."

"There were other barracks?" Donna asked.

"Oh yes, many. The barrack you were assigned depended on how you were designated, requiring one to wear a color-coded triangle, or *winkel,* identifying their category. Polish women wore red triangles, denoting their designation as political prisoner. Soviet prisoners, as well as German and Austrian communists, also wore red triangles. Prostitutes, lesbians, or women who refused to marry wore black triangles. Jewish women wore a yellow triangle. Jehovah's Witnesses wore the purple triangle. Green triangles were worn by criminals—many of whom became kapos. Each color-coded group was housed according to their assigned designation.

"Female members of the Polish underground, known as *The Walls,* are credited with preserving the last moments of Ravensbrück's operation. The rest of the camp documents, prior to the Polish underground involvement, were burned by escaping SS overseers. The fact these papers escaped the fire lends credibility to the likely event someone understood the endangered situation and acted before it was too late, before *all* records were destroyed."

"So, it must have been a Jewish woman who took these papers," Donna declared with a growing sense in her new theory.

"Not necessarily," Herta cautioned. "It could have been anyone, a member of the SS or a simple clerk, or anyone who wanted a keepsake of the camp to show their family and friends years later. Having said that, there is another gnawing thought."

"What is it?"

"These papers were included with birth and marriage certificates. So, in my opinion, this is personal."

Donna nodded in understanding. "I find it interesting the note accompanying this package was typed and not signed," Donna said while handing the note to Herta.

"Interesting. You are saying this note is not from your friend's sister, then? Your friend, Mr. Tandermann?"

"Yes. Why would his sister sign a letter with the first parcel, but not sign a letter with this mailing? I'm thinking someone else forwarded this information. Someone who is involved, but not willing to reveal him or herself."

"The box it came in does not reveal an address," Herta added, handling the box, "adding to the suspicion someone does not want to be revealed. I would advise you to search the archives of the United States Holocaust Memorial Museum. They have a surprising amount of information. Perhaps something might come of it."

"Where would I start?" Donna asked.

"I would start with the names on these sheets of paper. It may lead to nothing, but it is worth a try. You must remember, in the end many of the fleeing SS and guards blended into society, taking on new names and creative backgrounds to distance themselves from their involvement. I fear your task will not be an easy one. Let me know if I can be of further assistance."

CHAPTER TWENTY-ONE

"Our obligation is to give meaning to life and in doing so to
overcome the passive, indifferent life."

Elie Wiesel

Summer 1955 – Greenville, South Carolina

Ilse had been gone for nearly three years now, and the child was
progressing nicely, evidencing a loving personality. If ever there
was an old soul understanding the human condition at its core,
and providing subtle support beyond still young years, this child
was such.

The idea came to Ida slowly. At first she had rejected it with a
vengeance. It would, over time however, reintroduce itself, subtly
prodding, probing, reminding, until efforts to resist proved futile.
At last, she presented her proposal to the sisters. They were, at
first, shocked by the suggestion. Ida rushed to explain it in detail,
even providing a comprehensive outline of how it would unfold.
The sisters murmured among themselves, asked questions, refuted
arguments, and suggested why the plan would not work.

Ida, in return, answered each question, allayed every fear,
supported all pronouncements and declarations, and provided
assurances. In the end, she allowed weeks for the sisters to review and
argue their positions. After all, she presented to them a life-changing
proposal. They had every right to question. Having developed lives

beyond Ravensbrück, their brief years beyond the camps yielded the start of normalcy. Some had reconnected with family. Others were involved with lovers and made plans for a future, while still others were embarking on business ventures to support their livelihoods. Ida's suggestion and plea was bold and daring, incomprehensible in many respects, and yet all listened. They would argue, discuss, and then argue again. They would embrace, and then push each other away. So it went, the dynamics of a life-changing decision in play. Ida accepted all demonstrations of emotion and mental processing without question. It was a necessary part of the process, she concluded. What would she do if some refused her offer? Another plan had to be in play for that possibility.

In the end, all agreed. The impossible had been achieved. There were details, however; oh, the details! This is where Ida triumphed. It was always the "devil and the details." At this she would excel, leaving none unsupported, in question, or fearful. They would find their way. After all. They were sisters.

The idea to relocate to America didn't enter Ida's mind until receiving the letter from her aunt and uncle, forwarded by the Red Cross.

They begged her to join them. She rejected the offer in her heart, but never on paper, always holding out false hope she would come for a visit; a visit that would never occur. And yet, the idea of moving to America began to grow in her heart.

Many ideas were unsettling. This she knew. Since the end of World War II, 20 million people had relocated to other countries. Immigration became a major event in many lands, with Canada and Australia taking on a large measure of immigrants by invitation. In

Australia alone, 1.2 million Europeans would settle between 1949 and 1959.

The United States had a more restrictive policy based on the country of origin. Still, 250 thousand people immigrated to the United States between 1946 and 1960. Ida was among them, settling in Greenville, South Carolina in the summer of 1955. How she had chosen this once obscure town situated at the foothills of the Blue Ridge Mountains was an anomaly. She researched America and American cities and towns two years before the move. Happening upon an article on the South, she became enamored by the reference to cotton and cotton fields. Ever the gardener, she read with relish the history of cotton in the southern half of America and learned of Greenville, often referred to as the "Textile Center of the South" because of its rich history in cotton mills.

With the war's end, Greenville's economy accelerated, leaning heavily toward the expansion of city limits, and the establishment of Bob Jones University and Greenville Technical College, which joined Furman University as educational centers. Eventually an airport would be established. Land was plentiful. It was in the land Ida took special interest, as well as the colleges. Both would serve her long-range goals.

Her entry into the country with the child was without mishap. She planned well, with the assistance of Sarah Sonntag's brother, Rudolf, and sister, Frieda. They had unexplained connections, and while Ida never asked, she knew her identity, and that of the child, would be protected. They provided the necessary papers ensuring her and the child's entry into America. They gave her, in addition, something unanticipated. A list. Rudolf and Frieda explained what it was, never revealing how they came to acquire it. Ida nodded in understanding, certain this was not the only copy, and tucked it safely into her pocket. Before taking her leave, Ida embraced

Sarah Sonntag's siblings warmly. She regretted leaving these two dear friends and advocates.

In less than two weeks, Ida made her way to Greenville, South Carolina, and found a small rental property on the outskirts of the city. It would suit her needs and the child's temporarily. The weather was hot and humid, and while she knew this condition was necessary for growing cotton, it was beyond uncomfortable for someone so unaccustomed to it. The introduction of air conditioning was having a transformational effect on the country. Learning of this, Ida's first order of business was to obtain two window units for her rental house. One was placed in the one bedroom, and the other, a larger unit, was installed in the living room. The units made life bearable in the summer, to say the least.

The child, nearly fifteen years old, needed to be schooled. Ida was very particular on this point, researching the limited private schools the area provided. She found one to her liking associated with a small Jewish synagogue. The staff was impressed by the child's English and German-language skills. The child made friends effortlessly, engaging in sports and other school-related activities. Ida was relieved by the results. Though the Rabbi encouraged Ida to attend worship services at the synagogue, she politely kept her distance except for sending the child for religious instruction.

During school days, Ida studied the layout of Greenville and available tracts of land, as well as available access to roadways. Her vision, far-reaching and comprehensive, was essential for the good of all. She relied heavily on the child to translate the town's only newspaper into German, and while she was learning English in bits and pieces, it seemed it would not truly take root as a comfortable means of communication. She would continue to struggle with learning English.

Her intent to find land proved successful when one day, nearly six months after their move to Greenville, the child pointed to one inclusion in the day's newspaper obituaries. The deceased was the aged parent of an instructor at the synagogue. By chance, Ida encountered the instructor the next week when she was at the school for a parent-teacher progress report. Ida conveyed her condolences at the teacher's recent loss.

The serendipitous exchange proved eventful. The instructor expressed an intent to place a tract of land, left by her recently deceased parent, for sale. Ida inquired as to its location. It proved to be ideal. Four months later, Ida signed papers for the transfer of property, nearly one hundred acres, much of it timbered, with access to a proposed highway and easy transport into the city.

Her next endeavor was to secure a contractor to build two homes to start. When encountering the instructor at the local market some weeks later, she asked for the recommendation of a reputable home-builder. Upon receiving a name, Ida called the builder and they arranged to meet. Jacob Schmidt met Ida at the property site three days later.

He was not an especially handsome man; his manner quiet and reserved. His smile, however, was infectious, and his laughter was deep and from the heart. Ida remembered a time when she could laugh deeply, but it had ceased to be. Immediately taken with this balding man with the big Jewish nose and a hint of playfulness, she laid out the survey for the property on the hood of his truck and her development plan. He was taken aback.

"Such an ambitious endeavor," he said, eyeing her closely. "This will take money. Lots of money."

"I have the means," she replied, meeting his intense gaze.

He remained quiet for a time, perusing the survey and the proposed plan, looking alternately at it and then Ida. "You understand I will require a sizeable deposit for the first two homes. After that, we can review our business plan going forward. I must say, I am puzzled by all of this. I noticed your German accent. Germany is still in the throes of upheaval, economically and politically. How is it you have come here to this country with such means?"

"I see you are a curious man, Mr. Schmidt," Ida replied in German. "I present a business venture. I am not inviting questions regarding my finances. I can assure you the deposit and subsequent expenses will be met."

Jacob felt chagrined, yet he was impressed by her stalwart response. "Forgive me," he replied in German. "I came to America from Germany with nothing, like so many others, and have had to build my way to fragile recognition. So you can understand when I encounter someone from my country who has the means to have a dream realized, I question the source. It was wrong of me to do so. I offer my sincerest apology."

"Perhaps you can suggest a plat map for the remaining homes," Ida said, moving on to more acceptable business terrain.

Jacob, relieved they were back on business terms, replied professionally, "Of course. Let me spend a day or two examining the layout of the land. A study of the topography will help me in suggesting possible placement. The resources here are impressive. Other than homes, do you have any other plans for the property?"

The question allowed Ida to reveal her latent plans. "Yes. I would like to include a private cemetery on the far corner of the property away from the residential area. Another option would be to include a gathering house, a cabin of sorts, for entertaining and community discussion. There should also be a playground situated in a park-like setting. Can this be done?"

Jacob took a closer look at the survey. "There appears to be enough acreage. I see there is a medium-sized pond on the south end of the property. Perhaps this is where your cabin and playground should be situated."

The discussion ended with plans to meet the following week for review. Ida discerned Jacob was an honest man, hardworking, and reliable. She had had little interaction with males with the exception of her father and brothers. After the camps, there was little socialization for her, not being sure what to say or how to act. It seemed everyone around her had a circle of friends and family. Other than Ms. Kaiser and the child, her circle was non-existent. The sisters provided some companionship, of course bound as they were by common history and focus. Ida remained guarded and on high alert. The slightest noise or movement was an intrusion, fraught with suspicion and mistrust. Perhaps things would be different as she became more comfortable in America, her new home. In the meantime, she had a job to do and a child to protect and raise. Still, her thoughts turned to Jacob before falling off to sleep that night. Yes, she sensed he was a good man.

CHAPTER TWENTY-TWO

Donna surmised her search into the intent behind the first package would entail determining how the list of forty kapos related to the other list of numbers provided. Where she would start in such an endeavor remained a question. At last, she placed a call to Kathe Hohman, the translator at the United States Holocaust Memorial Museum who had assisted during their visit to Washington, D.C.

Kathe answered on the first ring. "Oh, I remember your visit," Kathe said after Donna identified herself. "Your friend was trying to find information about his sister, if I recall correctly. How is he coming with his search?"

"We are slow to put all the pieces together, I'm afraid," Donna answered.

"These matters can be difficult to understand. How can I be of help?"

"I know I'm asking a great deal, but if you were me, how would you go about tracking down the names of the kapos?"

"Oh dear. A mammoth job, I fear. Are you trying to determine if they are still alive?"

"I suppose I am," Donna replied, her path to answers made clear by the question. "If they are still alive, my search should reveal their current whereabouts."

"I would caution you about being too optimistic. Many overseers of the camps attempted to blend in with society, even changing their names to hide their past, even if it was a past that was free from blemish; a means of starting over, mind you." There was silence for a time before Kathe spoke again.

"It has occurred to me that some, but not all, may have been local people near the camps. In all likelihood, they returned to their homes. Have you searched the archives of the museum for the list of survivors?"

"Not yet," Donna answered, embarrassed she had not thought of this approach.

"I would suggest you review our records first. They are quite extensive. From there, you can inquire of relief agencies most often engaged in the rescue and relocation of the refugees at the time to see whether or not their records have a name or two."

"This gives me some direction," Donna said, somewhat relieved a plan of action was in play. Another nagging thought drove her to ask a most unorthodox question of Kathe. In so doing, the older woman, a camp survivor herself, was taken aback.

"Forgive me, but I was not prepared for this type of inquiry. I am not fully informed on this subject, but to answer your question with what I know to be true, in the immediate aftermath of Hitler's suicide, there were other notable suicides. Your question aligns with rumors from the time, never substantiated. The rumors died a slow death. I had forgotten all about them until now. I would be curious to know what basis you have for making such an inquiry. It is very unorthodox at this late date."

"Yes, I would think so," was all Donna said.

Kathe Hohman picked up on Donna's hesitance. "Perhaps you will share when you are ready. There are books written on the matter, many books, in fact. Some may prove useful to you."

"I will certainly consider looking into them."

"You understand, of course, any revelation of such a nature could bring unintended consequences."

"What do you mean?"

"Let me just say there are those who still wish to rid the world of any reminder of Hitler's regime."

Donna was stunned by the implication, but simply said. "Of course. Fortunately, as you say, they are just rumors."

Immersed in the archives provided by the museum, along with her own intense reading on the final days of the war in Berlin, Donna garnered a good understanding of the chaos and deplorable events that took place in the city and throughout Germany in those final days.

Most satisfying, however, was the measure of success she obtained in the arduous task of tracking down the forty names on the list titled *Kapos*. All the names were of women, but she suspected as much because of their being prisoners themselves in the all-female Ravensbrück camp. Not surprising, all on the list were now dead. In reviewing death certificates, some unsettling details surfaced. At first, she almost overlooked them, but upon closer scrutiny, there appeared to be a pattern among the deaths. One detail was immediately obvious. Donna had the scent of something sinister in play related to the list of numbers and names. She would keep her findings to herself for now. There was no point in revealing mere suspicion, but for Donna, the hunt was on.

CHAPTER TWENTY-THREE

"No one is as capable of gratitude as one who has
emerged from the kingdom of the night."

Elie Wiesel, Nobel Peace Prize Acceptance Speech, 1986

Summer 1956 – Greenville, South Carolina

Development of Ida's community was well underway. The
water and electric lines were installed and the road cut in,
with special consideration for an underground tunnel on
both sides of the street. She was pleased with the results. She and
Jacob conversed every day to address questions and details. Their
professional relationship was growing toward a friendship, having
spent enough time together to find a comfortable balance.

It wasn't too long before Ida moved into the first of the two
homes, purposely understated in its outward appearance. Each
house would be different from those built afterward.

At one point, Jacob offered a comment. "I understand the trend
is to create a sales office to parcel out the properties. Perhaps you
might consider this."

Ida replied, not even looking up from her review of the invoices
for the first and second homes. "All the homes are promised."

Jacob whipped his head in her direction. "You mean, *sold?* Are
you saying all these homes are already sold?"

Ida paused in her perusal to look up at Jacob and address the question. "In a manner of speaking. The homes, every one of them, have been spoken for. There will be no need for a sales office. They will be filled as quickly as you can build them."

"I don't understand," he replied, somewhat undone by the revelation. "How is this possible?"

Ida looked at Jacob from a position of warm friendship, a feeling new to her, and pleasant. Her response was kind. "I have been so involved with the project, I failed to include you in the particulars. You understand, of course, there are many who wish to come to America after the nightmare in Europe. I vowed that, when and if I was granted passage to America, I would sponsor other German refugees. This community is for that purpose."

"They're paying for this?" Jacob asked, aghast.

"In a manner of speaking."

"What does this mean…'In a manner of speaking?' Are they paying you for their homes? All twenty of them?"

Ida was careful not to reveal too much. "They have paid, I can assure you. Dearly."

Jacob looked at the woman he had taken a liking to. She was smart, very smart. Though small in stature, she was mighty in fortitude. He noted a strong streak of caution in any conversations that veered toward the personal. He wanted to know her better. He was mesmerized by her laughter, on those rare occasions she allowed herself to laugh. Her control of emotion was monumental. Who was she, really? What maelstroms was she harboring?

Changing the subject to the construction project to bring them on more level footing, he asked, "What do you plan to call this community, Ida? I can arrange for signage to be placed at the entrance."

Ida never hesitated for a moment in her reply, "Kaiser Commons."

"Very nice. The street name running through the village? It will be a private road. What name do I assign to it?"

"It shall be called Ilse Way."

Jacob sensed a deep personal determination in Ida's replies. Ida turned the subject to an entirely unexpected direction. "Jacob, what can you tell me about kit homes?"

"Why do you ask?" he replied, caught off guard.

"I have read about them. Would they accelerate our progress?"

"Does our progress need acceleration?" he inquired, surprised by the turn in conversation.

"To some degree. When I came here, I had a two-year plan. The first year has been largely used with the purchase of the land and property development. If I understand my research correctly, the next eighteen homes can be erected more quickly if they are kit homes. Is my understanding correct?"

"Yes," Jacob replied hesitantly. "I've never constructed one, but they have been very popular in the past."

"How do they work?"

"Essentially, each piece of lumber is pre-cut in the factory, numbered, and designed to fit into its particular place in the house."

"So, no measuring and cutting on site," Ida concluded. "That would speed things along."

"I would think so. The houses are standardized, but you have some options in design and floor plans. You would realize substantial cost-savings, I might add."

"I am more interested in the time factor. Can we have them all installed this year?"

"Eighteen homes, and the cabin?"

"Yes."

"This would require some discussion with the company."

"Tomorrow, then?" Ida persisted.

Jacob smiled at the tenacious women beside him. "You certainly don't allow any grass to grow under your feet, do you?"

The confused look on Ida's face made Jacob laugh heartily.

"What do you mean, 'grass grow under your feet'?" Ida asked innocently, enjoying the look of laughter on Jacob's face. How he glowed when he laughed.

"Here," he said, guiding her to his truck by her elbow. "Share a cup of coffee with me from my thermos and I'll explain this American expression."

Ida walked with Jacob, surprised his gentle touch had such an effect on her. She looked into his eyes as they walked and found he was looking back at hers. Their gaze locked, if only for a second, but an unspoken understanding passed between them all the same.

By fall of that year, six kit homes in varying degrees of readiness were under construction on firm foundations with twelve more on the way, as well as an additional structure that would serve as the community's gathering center, built in a cabin-type design by the pond. Ida was confident she could begin the process of marshalling the sisters to America until the homes were filled. Keeping in mind the needs of each sister, she took the liberty of assigning the homes herself to avoid confusion and conflict.

Building the community was affording Jacob positive exposure as a contractor, with many prospective homeowners coming by to view the progress of the development. It allowed him to submit bids on their plans, creating a backlog of work after Kaiser Commons was completed. Jacob and Ida were spending a great deal of time together discussing their progress. Their business relationship had grown into a deep personal friendship during the past two years, their comfort with each other evident in their tendency to tease and make fun of each other until both were speechless with laughter. For Jacob, he knew for some time he was in love with Ida. She was unlike any woman he had ever met, but she had gave no sign of interest in him beyond friendship.

Nonetheless, the couple established a movie night each week with dinner, a casual affair in which Ida insisted on paying for her own dinner, much to Jacob's consternation. He had little to no dating experience, and remained at a loss as to how to take their relationship to a more romantic and personally involved level. At last he made up his mind to make his feelings known, regardless of the outcome.

When the check arrived for their dinner that week, Ida reached out for it as usual to calculate what she owed, but Jacob placed a firm hand over hers.

"Not this time," he said quietly. "From this point on I pay for our meals," he continued, taking both of her hands in his.

Ida cocked her head in confusion. "I don't understand."

Jacob drew in a deep breath, clearly nervous, sweat beading on his forehead. "I need to make my position clear, Ida. Forgive me for taking so long to share with you my feelings, but you should know that I'm in love with you, and have been from almost the start. I can't assume you are ready to return my love, but my heart is just begging to pay for your dinner and your movies from here into eternity, and then some. I wish for you to consider a future with me, Ida, as my wife. Have I gone too far, too soon?"

Jacob gazed steadily into Ida's eyes seeking an answer, hoping for the best but prepared for the worst. She was clearly surprised and remained silent for some time.

Finally, she answered. "I would be untruthful if I were to say you have had no effect on me. You are a good man, Jacob, and I both respect and admire you."

"Is this a good thing?" he asked jokingly, while holding his breath.

"Oh, yes," she replied with a gentle voice, returning the embrace of his hands in hers. "You have softened my heart, allowing me to think about love and all it means. You should know I am naturally distrusting, so my acceptance will be slower than most. Can you put up with my delayed response?"

With that, Jacob stood up and reached across the table to kiss Ida gently on the lips. The impact on Ida was powerful, the full measure of his love transferred in a single kiss. When she didn't resist, he kissed her again, longer this time. For Ida, there was no one else in the room, no bustling or chatter of other patrons conversing or laughing, no orders being yelled out to the kitchen, no music in the background, just this moment of oneness. Finally answering her, Jacob returned, "I can put up with anything except your rejection or indifference."

"You shall have neither," Ida said lovingly.

⁓

There was still so much he didn't know about her, but he was willing to learn. He perceived there was a deep, hurtful past she had not revealed. Would she ever trust him enough to share her pain?

It was the planning of the cemetery that provided an occasion for a bit of Ida's past to be revealed. She was very particular on its layout, almost obsessive in its fabrication.

"I can have signage prepared as we work on the layout. What would you like to name the cemetery?"

"It shall be called Sonntag Memorial Garden," was Ida's quiet, and almost reverent, reply.

Within weeks, the signage was in place complete with a symbol designating it as a Jewish cemetery. Ida watched intently as the grand archway of her own design was put into place, complete with its name *Sonntag Memorial Garden*. She stood on a misty morning observing its installation almost reverently and cried until the process was complete.

Jacob could only stand by and hold her hand, not understanding how much this single act affected his beloved. Knowing not to prod until she was ready, he could already tell the cemetery held great meaning for Ida. He often found her there later in their lives sitting among the markers of the deceased, or setting flowers at the sites of those she held in high esteem.

Shortly after the completion of the cemetery layout and installation, a special package arrived from Germany. Ida placed it on the far corner of her kitchen counter without explanation or fanfare, but Jacob knew it was something significant, for she became quiet when it arrived and remained so for several days.

They developed a routine to meet for lunch at the pond each day, weather permitting. Jacob built a picnic table for the two of them, placing it in the shade of a grand old oak tree near the pond's edge. They would take turns bringing food for the day. This afternoon it was Jacob's turn to bring lunch. He did so and waited for Ida, an unusual occurrence because she was always there before him, as he was often detained by questions from subcontractors. When she had still not arrived an hour later, he became concerned. He went to her house, but she was not home. This was totally out of character for her. By chance, he went to the cemetery. There he spotted her sitting quietly, wrapped in a silence only she understood, with the package gripped tightly in her lap and another beside her on the bench. He was unnerved by her pained expression. Approaching slowly, he felt as if he were intruding on a most reverent moment. His feet upon the gravel announced his arrival. Ida slowly turned toward him, her eyes drenched in tears, swollen by the memories of a painful past.

Jacob sat beside her, powerless and helpless all at once. He could only share his feelings. "I would give my life to take away your pain, spend my last breath to infuse you with hope, wrap you in my devotion to give you a reason to laugh again. Trust me, Ida. Trust me with your past."

Ida slowly began to share with Jacob her history. "The box on my lap is filled with the ashes of my mother and father, retrieved in recent months from the riverbed beside Ravensbrück at my request by my dear friend, Rudolf Coble, and his sister, Frieda Brier. It is a symbolic gesture.

"I don't understand," Jacob returned quietly, though his heart was beating wildly.

Ida turned to look at Jacob, seeing the innocence on his face, the confusion, and the love. How she wanted to spare this man her past, but in doing so she knew it would get in the way of their future. This was the time. The time to tell the man she loved her history.

"Jacob, I am a survivor of Ravensbrück, one of the concentration camps outside of Berlin during Hitler's rule. Both my parents died in the camps. My father died at Camp Vught. My mother died in Ravensbrück. I entered Camp Vught at the age of thirteen and was liberated from Ravensbrück at the age of fifteen.

"My God!"

"The ovens of Ravensbrück spilled out the ashes of thousands of the dead into the air, only to have them settle in the lakebed nearby. To those of us who survived, but left loved ones, the lake is sacred, a reminder of the horror, a place to retrieve a facsimile of those torn from us in such a brutal fashion."

At this point Ida began to cry again. The floodgates of memory opened, her tears evolved into a mournful and soulful unveiling of long-contained grief held tightly until now. Her lamentations, linked with cries for her mother and father, were more than Jacob could endure. He could never have imagined such a release of trapped emotion. Ida was swallowed by her grief, by an anguish she had locked way inside all these years. Jacob drew her gently into his arms, holding her body now racked with uncontrollable sobbing, as if her soul were attempting to free itself from an ugly purgatory. In the process, her face looked twisted and stretched in expressions of inexplicable pain as her calls for "Papa" and "Mamma" continued. She went on this way for some time, with Jacob all the while uttering soothing words, stroking her gently, kissing her softly, and keeping her in his embrace.

At last her sobbing quieted, replaced by sniffling as she now lay across Jacob's lap in utter exhaustion. For some time Jacob didn't dare speak. When he did, his voice was soft, ever so soft. "What is your wish, Ida? Tell me, my love."

Finally, she lifted her head to face him, her eyes swollen from her outcry. "I prepared a place for them. Not only for them, but for my Ms. Kaiser. I wish to settle them here, in this place."

Jacob was moved by Ida's words to the point of tears. "This is why you named the development as you did, to honor Ms. Kaiser. I understand. Then, it shall be done," Jacob said with assurance. "Tell me about your Ms. Kaiser, Ida. I wish to know all there is about you and her."

Ida smiled, knowing she would never reveal all to Jacob, but this time she could accommodate his request to a degree. How loyal he was in his devotion. She sighed before sharing. "When the camp was liberated, I was beyond weakness and near dying. The rumors were ripe of the nearness of the Red Army and the Americans. I remember lying on the *appellplatz* along with hundreds of others to wait. At one point, I opened my eyes to look at the sky. It seemed to be snowing. How could this be? It was April. Then I knew. The debris raining down on us were the ashes from the ovens spewing remains. The Germans were so intent on hiding their madness, they doubled their efforts at the incinerators. Then I blacked out and awoke days later in a makeshift hospital set up in the camp by Swedish relief agencies. After a time, I began my slow return to an approximation of health and was pronounced well enough to travel. But where to go? I had no one.

"My only option was to go back to the woman who for almost two years hid my family from the SS behind a wall in her home, Ilse Kaiser. I had no idea, however, if she was still alive, for she, her sister, and their elderly father were taken prisoner by the SS for hiding Jews. I discovered later that her sister and father died in the camps as well. Even if I found her, I had no idea if she would take me in, and yet it was my only option. It took weeks to travel to her home in the Netherlands. It was dangerous travel. Rumors were rampant of the Soviet Army's vicious treatment and rape of women regardless of age, however, I prevailed and eventually found the home of Mr. Kaiser. She had returned and gave me a home until her death."

"And the child?" Jacob probed.

"The child is an orphan. It would have been unforgivable not to provide a home for one so small at the time," Ida answered benignly. "I guard this soul with my life."

Jacob was sitting beside Ida on one of the many concrete benches placed around the cemetery. In time she rose, wiping her tear-swept eyes before stepping toward the concrete structure with the two drawers. One was marked *Olaf and Hinkle Tandermann*, the other *Ilse Kaiser*, with dates of birth and death. Jacob watched as she reverently placed the urn with her parents' ashes in their drawer, and then proceeded to place Ms. Kaiser's ashes in the other drawer. She then bent her head in benediction. Jacob never saw Ida offer any gesture of worship until now.

Having completed the task, Ida turned to Jacob. "It is done. Their placement is complete. They are home among friends and family, at last."

"Do you not wish the Rabbi to preside?"

"There is plenty of time for such things. Later, perhaps."

CHAPTER TWENTY-FOUR

Donna knew she had a tiger by the tail, but didn't know how big the tiger was. Several issues remained, nagging details, and whenever she experienced this kind of troubling gap she knew she was near to finding something.

In her ever-inquiring mind, there remained four questions. The first related to the two lists in the first parcel, and how they correlated with one another. For that question, she knew she was near to having an answer. The second question centered on where Gavin's sister, Ida Ann Tandermann, went after leaving Ravensbrück and coming to America in 1955. In Donna's mind, there was a ten-year gap in this woman's life requiring investigation.

The third question had two parts. How the first parcel correlated with the second one, and who sent the second one.

A fourth question, which she at first tried to ignore, but which was etched in her thoughts all the same, was related to a recent observation that left a queer impression. Initially she thought nothing of it, but as she delved deeper into the final days of the Holocaust and the Nazi leaders, the hold it had on her grew in strength.

For the last several weeks she had been wholly absorbed in the final days of the German regime, with leaders now in bunkers, and the capital city under constant bombardment by Russian and American forces. She was certain if she dug deeply enough, she would find something someone had written that would provide the answer to her puzzle. The best place to start, she had determined, were the museums and memorials of the United States dedicated to the Holocaust. To her surprise, she discovered twenty-six states hosted museums or memorials to either the dead or the survivors. In all, she found fifty-six memorials in the United States, but the worldwide number of tributes were staggering. Donna confined her search to museums in the United States. If need be, she would branch out beyond that, but hoped she wouldn't have to go further.

Donna's persistence was rewarded in her third week while she was researching in the archives of one of the smaller museums. In an offhanded manner, the writer of the piece she was reading claimed to have been present and covertly involved in a ruse. Donna was stunned, but needed another such claim for substantiation. She continued delving into the archives of various museums and by chance, found another claim, this one dubious, but a claim nonetheless. In both instances, the person making the claim was dead, and had been for some time, but their personal commitment and responsibility at the time made Donna believe what they had written. If true, this was the bombshell of the century. Her quandary was whether to expose her find. She decided to judiciously examine the question over time.

Having satisfied this major point, Donna then delved looked for documentation of the whereabouts of Ida Ann Tandermann during the ten-year period from her departure from Ravensbrück to her immigration to America. In doing so, she contacted the Swedish relief organization established in Berlin after the city's collapse, hoping that Ida sought to contact other displaced relatives. There was no reply for several weeks, but when she did receive it, it was comprehensive. Indeed, there was an Ida Ann Tandermann who filed a displaced person's affidavit with the American Red Cross in Berlin, looking for her aunt and uncle. Donna jumped for joy when a contact address for Ida was part of the information; Haarlem, Netherlands. Further research revealed the family associated with this address was part of the resistance movement, hiding Jews at their own expense in a top-floor bedroom, only to be discovered by the SS. A remaining member of the family, Ilse Kaiser, survived the concentration camp experience at Camp Vught and later Ravensbrück.

Donna determined Ida and Ilse must have discovered they were victims of the same camp, at nearly the same time, but in different compounds. Their paths would fail to cross though, in the wretched environment of Ravensbrück.

Satisfied with her search thus far, Donna decided to turn her attention to the list of numbers and the list entitled *Kapos*. How were they related? They must be related, she thought, or else they would not have been included in the parcel. Donna had a sense Gavin's sister, Ida, was cunning and wily. The fact that she arranged for these papers to be forwarded was an indication of something in her past she wanted revealed. Again, Donna spent considerable time researching the names on the list through the archives of the American museums. It yielded, in time, some results, but not enough to be comprehensive. She needed to extend her search to German sources, but before doing so she called her friend, Herta Cohen.

After sharing with Herta her effort to track down the kapos listed, she asked Herta where she would start if she were Donna.

"It seems to me," Herta began thoughtfully, "most of the kapos would be looking for lost or displaced relatives themselves. You may just go back to the relief agencies present at the time to see whether or not any on your list appear on their lists, and then follow the trail."

"Yes! That is exactly how I shall proceed."

"It will take time. If I recall correctly, you have forty names. The task is daunting, my child, but there is no other one up to the task."

Donna plodded on, using Herta's suggestion. Her effort yielded surprising finds as to where most of the kapos went after they garnered their freedom. They were scattered across five countries. With that information, she obtained the death certificates for as many as she could, at least three quarters of those listed. Placing them in the order of date of death, she studied them over a two-week period with growing suspicion. Her shock at the pattern that appeared rattled her beyond anything she encountered to date as a forensic psychiatrist.

Ken was away at a law enforcement seminar and would not be returning until the following evening. She needed to speak with him. He was always her voice of reason. That evening she called his cell phone.

"Hey, beautiful," he answered on the first ring.

"How's the seminar?" she asked, feigning interest, but anxious to share her quandary.

"Not too bad. I've made some great connections. How's the search coming?"

"Now, that's the thing. It has been revealing and unsettling." With that, Donna shared her findings, all of them.

Ken grew quiet.

"Are you there?" she finally asked.

"Yes, I'm here," he returned.

"Did you hear what I said?"

"I heard every word, and wish I hadn't. Do you know what this revelation will do to Gavin and his nephew?"

"I didn't start this, Ken. Gavin's sister did."

"Seems she had a strange sense of humor."

"I don't think its humor at all. I think it is a wish for absolution from her family for her estrangement and secrets all these years. I think it is an explanation, an excuse, a story behind the story. For the first time in a long time, I don't know what to do with my findings. Ken, tell me what to do. I don't want to expose Gavin to this evidence and where it points."

"Back up, sweetie. We don't know the full story or her intent behind sharing what she did. Perhaps there is more to learn that isn't so dark."

Donna sighed. "I hope you're right. Come home. I need you to help me figure out a way to cope with this thing."

CHAPTER TWENTY-FIVE

"Hope is like peace. It is not a gift from God. It is
a gift only we can give one another."

Elie Wiesel

Greenville, South Carolina - 1956

Ida changed after her personal outpouring at the cemetery. To
Jacob, it was an unmistakable shift. She became more open,
more available, and even more trusting of him from that point
forward. For Ida, establishing a final resting place for her dear ones
and sharing memories with Jacob enabled her to surrender fully
to the enduring and soulful love of her dear Jacob. In so doing, a
floodgate of yearning was unleashed that, up until now, was reticent
and dubious.

Several weeks after the cemetery experience, they were eating
their dinner while conversing quietly, but Jacob noticed a light
in Ida's eyes, as though the dark corners of her soul had been
illuminated. As was their custom, he helped her with the dishes
before leaving for his home for the night. After he gathered his
jacket, she placed her arms lovingly around him.

"Stay," was all she said.

He held her for a moment. "For the night?" he asked.

"Forever," was her soft reply.

Before the break of dawn, the hours unleashed a deluge of
lovemaking for the two lonely hearts, especially for Ida. She gave

herself willingly and unconditionally, seeking to satisfy Jacob without any boundaries. She had finally found love, a forever love, and accepted it with a profound and undying gratitude. That night began a journey of lifelong adoration, during which they raised two children, a son and a daughter. Years later, after Jacob's passing, Ida said to one of her granddaughters, "Until you find true, abiding, and trusting love, you have not lived. I was a lucky one."

The arrival of the sisters to America began in the fall and arrivals continued over a six-month period until all had settled into their new homes and country. Jacob was introduced as the one who built their homes, but they would soon discover his relationship with Ida, for he was observed entering her home in the evenings and not leaving until morning. At the same time, they were greeted by a transformed Ida. Gone was the deep lines of consternation across her forehead, along with her furtive glances of suspicion. They were replaced instead by a buoyancy in spirit. A child-like wonder danced in her eyes, as if seeing life and finding love for the first time. America had been good to Ida, they concluded, and they were pleased.

In turn, Ida was good to the sisters. Some brought family with them, others their spouses or lovers. Everything was riding on Ida's assurances of well-being. All were thrilled when presented with their homes, elated that such a blessing was bestowed upon them for the rest of their lives.

Jacob observed the closeness of the women and that conversation often quieted upon his unexpected approach. There was a secret among them, he was sure. They were especially happy to see the child and were attentive and protective toward the young one.

This surprised Jacob the most. Though he was pleased by it all, he wondered about the circumstances that had brought these people together.

The sisters agreed with and were supportive of Ida's plan for each family to contribute toward the good of the community. She set up a committee to oversee the responsibilities. The grounds were large enough for a small farm and garden. The committee assigned some residents to the farm, others to the garden, and the rest to maintain the grounds, pond, and cabin. Ida envisioned that the community would be self-sufficient wherever possible. Disputes and disagreements were handled by the committee on those rare occasions.

The time came for Jacob and Ida to marry. The sisters and their families were jubilant at the prospect and suggested a weekend-long celebration. Ida agreed the Rabbi should marry them. This seemed to please Jacob. She would do whatever it took to satisfy this man who filled her being with love, laughter, and renewal.

Two ideas came to Ida sometime before the wedding. She set about to write a letter to put one idea in action, and spoke to the Rabbi concerning the other.

The day before the wedding, a limousine pulled into Ida's driveway. Eagerly anticipating its arrival, she had been pacing back and forth and watching from their door. When it finally arrived, Ida ran from the house. She had told Jacob special guests would be arriving from Germany, but little else. He joined Ida, watching her hug her two guests with unbridled joy.

"It was kind of you to invite us, Ida," Rudolf Coble said while hugging Ida. "Your letters have been so welcoming."

"Yes, an unexpected pleasure," Frieda Brier offered in agreement. "We wouldn't miss this occasion for anything in the world." Ida had not shared with either her plan for the weekend after the wedding.

Ida and Jacob were married late Saturday evening, with the celebration going on past midnight. The child served as Ida's maid of honor. Jacob's brother was best man. The sisters outdid themselves in tribute to the happy couple with food, music, dancing, and even fireworks as the clock struck midnight. After the fireworks, Ida addressed her family, friends, and guests. "You couldn't have made this day any happier," she said. "Having you all present enhances an already perfect day. I hope the celebration will continue into tomorrow. I am inviting all of you to join us at the gates of the cemetery tomorrow evening. We have unfinished business I trust you will assist me in completing. It will require your blessing."

She had told no one of this plan, not even Jacob. His face reflected the surprise of the sisters and guests. The next evening, however, the community was at the entrance of the cemetery. The gates of the cemetery had been locked the night before. Ida and Jacob went by the cabin where Rudolf and Frieda were staying, and escorted them to the entryway of the cemetery. For the first time, Rudolf and Frieda understood the two-fold purpose of their visit. Ida addressed the crowd. Looking up at the sign, Ida spoke mainly to the sisters. "Last evening I spoke of unfinished business. Wouldn't you agree it is now time to honor the woman who made this all possible?" Those who understood, heartily applauded, nodding in agreement.

At that point, a vehicle came toward the driveway leading to the entrance of the cemetery. The Rabbi exited. Ida acknowledged him with a smile and continued to address the crowd. "This has been a happy time for Jacob and me, blissfully happy. I would be remiss, however, if I did not acknowledge the gift of Sarah Sonntag. It is because of her we were able to come to America to begin a new life and be given the chance to give back, in some way, the untold blessing we have received because of this wise and wonderful woman. With that in mind, I have invited the Rabbi to bless our cemetery, Sonntag Memorial Garden. Do I have your approval?"

The crowd applauded and cried in enthusiasm and agreement, especially the sisters who knew the import of Ida's comments. Rudolf and Frieda were moved beyond words, as the gates of the cemetery were unlocked, allowing the supporters to enter. Unknown to Jacob, Ida arranged for lighting to be placed throughout the grounds and for landscaping that included flowering trees and bushes to provide beauty in every season. Flowers were everywhere, their color and scents tantalizing the senses. The Rabbi allowed time for the group to wander about, taking in the sacred grounds before calling the guests to order. They gathered around him reverently. He then offered a prayer that even Ida could endorse. The occasion was especially moving. The sisters cried, embracing each other in the aftermath. Many sought out Rudolf and Frieda in an extended show of gratitude.

Ida called them to order once again. "These grounds, and the acreage beyond upon which our homes rest, are to be honored, but especially these grounds. The Sonntag Memorial Garden is for the exclusive use of our community and will not be opened to any other for the next one hundred years. By then, we will all have made good use of it." The crowd laughed and applauded the decree. "Even then," she continued, "a foundation has been established for its continuing care. I have asked the Rabbi to bless us now as a community."

The Rabbi smiled at Ida before doing so. He had been surprised when she requested his services, since she did not go to temple. He wondered what motivated such displays of thoughtfulness and devotion to these people. He did not know the answer, and neither did Jacob.

The time soon came for a decision to be made on the child's education beyond high school. Ida knew the course to be taken, but she wanted the teenager to agree as well. The child was astute, and highly perceptive, adding to Ida's long-term goal. Before long, the child enrolled in a nearby college and willingly pursued an education in economics and accounting, leading to a master's degree. This was a relief to Ida, who was ever mindful of the community's future.

The ensuing years were good to Ida, undoing the insult from the past. She raised two healthy children, adored her husband, and enjoyed rewarding experiences with the sisters. The child, for who she had accepted responsibility many years ago was a further blessing, enhancing her life beyond her expectation. There were few worries for her, only blessings. She would finally gain an understanding that they were everywhere if you looked for them. Even when she wasn't looking, blessings were all around, nudging at her soul, piquing her interest, nibbling at her awareness.

Stripping herself of her past was achieved, she knew, through an enduring love. In Jacob, she had found her salvation, her truest blessing. From her marriage through the rest of her days, her heart was light, and her steps buoyant.

CHAPTER TWENTY-SIX

Donna had a decision to make. Pacing over her findings, and more than a little uncomfortable with the results, she contemplated not only the undoubtedly surprising revelation, but Gavin's reaction to it as well. What were the odds that receiving a parcel could have such an impact? Donna could make the findings public, or confine the audience to a trusted few. She chose the latter. In reviewing what she knew of Ida's history, she concluded it was one thing to endure the torture of Hitler's concentration camps, but a different matter to be restored to wholeness. Donna's intuition strongly suggested that Ida Ann Tandermann Schmidt ended up on the side of wholeness.

Donna appreciated that current culture was far removed from events seventy-five years in the past. Her decision, then, with Ken's support, was to share her findings with a very few. But who? Gavin was an integral part of all this. After all, his sister had chosen to send him the parcel, for reasons now becoming clear. Donna's suspicion that Ida had a carefully contrived plan was now starting to become apparent. Donna decided to include Gavin in her review. But who else? Who else would preserve the secret?

Upon Ken's return home from his conference, she approached him with her decision. After thoroughly reviewing it with him, she sat back awaiting his feedback.

"Of all the cases you have been involved with, this is the most sensitive," he said with conviction. "Are you sure you have your facts straight?" he asked, ever the detective.

"Ken, I've gone over it a dozen times. I wish I were wrong, but I'm afraid I'm not. What would you do, if you were me?"

Ken sighed deeply before responding. "I would tell Gavin only, and let him decide who else should know."

Donna sat back, struck by the simplicity and reasonableness of Ken's reply. Of course! Tell the person most affected and let that person decide how to proceed.

Several days later, Donna made a call to Gavin. He answered on the second ring. "Hey, gal! Carole tells me you have been rather quiet lately. Everything okay?"

"Yes. We're both fine," Donna said, though she was ill at ease. "Gavin, I need some time with you alone. It's about your sister."

"I don't like the sound of your voice. Do I need to worry?"

"No. You don't need to worry. You just need to know. Can we meet, privately?

"Of course. This sounds ominous."

Two days later, Gavin crossed the country road to Donna's home after Carole left for the morning to address business related to her cafés. He didn't tell his wife about the meeting, another departure from his regular behavior. To Donna, he looked more than a bit apprehensive.

Gavin was surprised to find Ken coming out of the back room. "Shouldn't you be catching the bad guys?" Gavin asked, hoping to lighten the encounter.

"I'll catch them this afternoon," Ken replied with a slight smile.

"Let's sit on the back porch. It's such a lovely morning," Donna suggested.

When they settled themselves, Gavin spoke, "Tell me what's going on. First you call and want a private meeting, and then I see Ken is here. I assume this is for support."

"More or less," Ken replied. "I'll let Donna share her findings. You'll understand when she finishes."

Gavin looked at Donna. "Let's have it. What have you unearthed?"

For the next hour or more, Donna shared with Gavin her initial concerns, and doubts, along with her approach to her research and her discovery. She revealed every detail, entertaining questions from Gavin and occasionally Ken. Gavin's facial expressions changed with each revelation, lines of surprise, shock, and concern etched across his forehead and eyes. His voice faltered at times.

When Donna finished she sat back exhausted and a bit apprehensive that Gavin would find fault with her findings.

"Could you be wrong?" he asked in a subdued, almost grief-stricken tone.

"I could only hope, but I don't think so," Donna returned quietly.

Gavin didn't respond for some time. Ken and Donna stole glances at each other, both growing uncomfortable in the lingering silence. Ken was about to say something when Gavin spoke.

"Carole must be told. I'll speak with her tonight. David as well. Immediately," he said with effort. "Donna, would you arrange a meeting for David and the two of us as quickly as possible? I would rather it be in Greenville."

"What about Carl's daughters?" Donna asked.

"I think not. If what you have shared is true, we must keep this confidential."

⁂

After dinner that evening, Carole called Donna. "I've been expecting your call," was all Donna said.

"Gavin has gone to bed early. He is exhausted. He told me everything. Do you have some time to talk tonight?"

"Of course I do," Donna replied.

Carole appeared within minutes. The women retreated to the backyard. The evening was unfolding a lovely summer presentation. Creatures of the night were making their presence known by subtle sounds and nuances blanketing the yard and wooded area beyond. There was a wisp of a breeze, signaling a shower coming before morning.

Comfortably settled, Donna closed her eyes briefly, taking in the scent of the evening. "How nature calms the soul," she thought to herself.

"Gavin and I talked," Carole began. "I can't imagine what this is doing to you."

Donna opened her eyes to look at her best friend in surprise. "Me? I am simply the bearer of bad news."

Carole smiled slightly and shook her head. "I know you, girlfriend. Trust me. You wouldn't have burdened Gavin with false supposition. You've built your reputation on your sound research and competent analysis. If you feel something is amiss, then something is amiss. Gavin will get through this with our support. I'm afraid this has been a heavy weight for you to bear, though."

Donna was relieved to have her friend's support. She began to share honestly. "There is a point in my process, which I haven't begun to understand mind you, where I despise my nagging thoughts. Often they are too awful to consider, too fraught with inhumanity. Those are the days I wish I were on a beach somewhere in the Caribbean making passionate love to Ken."

Carole chuckled. "Too bad you can't snap your fingers and make it happen!"

The women laughed, as they had a thousand times before, understanding and accepting each other completely. Donna, finally gathering herself, continued, "Then there is this 'snap' in my brain. This is the only way I can explain it. It's as if my mind comes to attention, and gathers all the detail and the undefined impressions and rolls it into a possible scenario. Then the hunt is on and I'm compelled, driven, and dogged until I have all the answers, some of which I would rather not have."

"How do you handle the outcome? It has to come at a personal price," Carole asked having wondered about it over the years of observing her friend professionally.

Donna looked frankly at Carole. "All the 'blabber' when authorities talk about compartmentalizing your feelings is just that—blabber. For me, it's initially weathering the shock of where the hunt is taking me. I get drawn in to the personal side of the investigation, the what-ifs, and then the possible outcomes. Once the hunt is under way and justified, then the pitbull in me engages. That is when my juices start flowing and I bite down and don't let go until I have all the answers."

"At which stage are you in this business with Gavin's sister?"

"I'm in the bite-down stage, where I don't let go until I have all the answers."

It was an early morning phone call, but Donna was determined to get it out of the way.

"Good morning, Donna. So good to hear from you. Is everything all right?" David Schmidt said cheerily, despite the early morning hour.

"Good morning, David. Yes, everything is fine. Are Corrine and your family well?" Donna asked politely, while chafing at the bit to share the real reason for her call.

"Yes, we're good."

"Forgive me for calling so early, but Uncle Gavin and I would like to come to Greenville. Some history has been unearthed regarding your mother. It's only right that I impart it to you as soon as possible, and your uncle agrees."

"Can you tell me what it is? Should I involve Uncle Carl's daughters?"

"In answer to your second question, no, Uncle Carl's daughters should not be included at this time."

"Is this something I need to worry about, Donna?"

"No, David. It is history. Simply history, although somewhat surprising. I want to include you in the findings."

"I understand," David said hesitantly, "but I am confused."

"I completely understand. I will explain it all, but you must agree our meeting is just between you, Corrine, Uncle Gavin, and myself for now."

David became silent, trying to figure out this twist in events. "Does my uncle have knowledge of the information you want to share with me?"

"Yes. In fact, it was his suggestion I call and set up a meeting."

"When do you hope to arrive?"

"This coming weekend. Is that too soon?"

"No, I don't think Corrine has anything planned." He then had a thought. "Donna, we have a cabin on the property. It's used as a

180

community center most of the time, but it has two bedrooms. I can reserve them for you. Does that sound good?"

Donna was pleased by David's offer. "That's very kind of you, David. Yes, we will stay there if the cabin is available. If not, we can stay where we stayed last time."

"I'll look into it and confirm it with you."

"David, you'll keep our meeting confidential?"

"Yes. I have to ask, though, and I hope you're not offended, but are you sure all this secrecy is necessary?"

Donna smiled, momentarily entertained by the innocence of the David's question, knowing it would turn out to be an overwhelming revelation. Donna replied, "I'll let you be the judge after our meeting."

CHAPTER TWENTY-SEVEN

Gavin and Donna arrived well before nightfall on Friday, meeting David and Corrine at the cabin located on the far end of the small neighborhood called Kaiser Commons. Donna noted the simplicity of the community with one road and twenty houses, ten on each side of the street. It was a lovely layout, each home distinctive in design and color and well maintained.

As they exited the vehicle, their hosts greeted them warmly. The Schmidts had a dog with them.

"Who is this beautiful creature?" Donna inquired. She loved animals and immediately sensed the dog was safe to pet. The dog wagged its tail in welcome. "He is magnificent, David," she remarked while rubbing the animal behind the ears. "What's his name?"

"He was my mother's dog. We adopted him when she passed. His name is Katche. "

"An interesting name," Donna returned, still petting the animal.

"Every dog my mother-in-law ever owned was named Katche. Go figure. I guess she didn't want to spend money on re-personalizing the water dishes," Corrine quipped. They all laughed.

Ushered into the cabin, Donna and Gavin were taken with the

warm ambience it projected. It was truly a log cabin, with a wrap-around porch, complete with rocking chairs. Inside, a cabin-like fragrance greeted them, borne of years of log burning in the stately fireplace. The rooms transmitted a feel-good invitation from years of entertainment and celebration. Donna was enraptured by the feeling, welcoming a respite before the distasteful task ahead of her began.

"David tells me you have already had supper, but there are drinks and snacks of every sort in the kitchen should you wish. We will bring breakfast sandwiches in the morning," Corrine graciously told them.

"I'll make the coffee," Gavin offered. "Carole sent us off with some of her best."

⊙≫⊘

While enamored by the surroundings, the circumstances that brought them to visit David and Corrine disturbed Donna, allowing her little sleep through the night. She mentally reviewed her findings, looking for any reason to offer an excuse of mistaken facts.

The morning banter among the four over breakfast centered on David's warm memories of his childhood. His recitals were not making Gavin and Donna's job easier.

Finally, Gavin broached the subject. He cleared his throat. "David, Corrine, as you know, there is some history regarding your mother you should be aware of."

"Other than her being a Holocaust survivor?" Corrine asked.

Gavin considered the question carefully before answering. "Yes, beyond her camp experience." Gavin then looked at Donna who simply nodded in confirmation. "I will turn this discussion over to

Donna. She has unearthed much of what you are about to hear," he said. He then sat back with a sick feeling in his stomach.

Donna gathered her thoughts and began a slow, but methodical unveiling of history. "David, your mother was, indeed, a Holocaust survivor. It is the aftermath of her experience that drew my interest."

"I don't understand," David replied, reaching for Corrine's hand.

Donna paused, quickly assessing the effect her next sentence would have on this man who clearly loved his mother. "It is my conviction that your mother had a secret life after the camps. It is also my belief that she was allied with others."

"What do you mean a secret life?" Corrine asked.

Donna struggled for the right words. Finally, she went for broke. "There is no easy way to say this, so I'll just tell you what I have uncovered. Your mother was part of an effort to eliminate those who provided oversight in the camps, possibly as many as forty."

David's face turned red, taking on an ungodly scowl, his fists balled in fury. "Eliminate? What are you saying? What do you mean eliminate?"

Donna froze, and looked at Gavin. They then heard David begin to laugh. "You had me for a second there, Donna. I actually thought you were accusing my mother of something sinister," he said through his laughter.

Donna swallowed hard before responding. "I'm not kidding, David. The evidence is almost overwhelming that your mother, along with other women detainees from the camp, formed an alliance, a vigilante group of sorts, to kill those responsible for their suffering."

Corrine's hand went to her mouth in an effort to stifle a sob. "No! No! You are mistaken! The woman we knew was a pillar of the community, a saint. There is no way she could be part of such an undertaking. Our children adored her. You have the wrong woman, Donna."

"You will need to present your evidence," David blurted in heated response, "and it had better be beyond question."

Donna looked at Gavin. His face was white. She reached shakily into her briefcase and pulled out a portfolio of papers. For the next two hours she painstakingly went over the evidence, providing proof at every juncture, substantiated with documents, some more than seventy years old, and answering questions as her listeners wept, including Gavin. When she concluded, there was silence in the room. She herself, was spent, the emotional effort more wrenching then she had anticipated. She had asked herself many times if she could just bury her findings and not reveal them, to allow this family to continue none the wiser. After all, wasn't there a saying that ignorance is bliss? Perhaps the blissful state of Ida's offspring should not be disturbed. Then again, she wondered, why send a package to Gavin, and another to Carl's family? Ida, Donna reasoned, wanted to reveal her past.

David, wiping his eyes and blowing his nose, finally spoke. "This will take some time to digest."

Donna, observing the pained expression, not only on his face, but also on Corrine's and Gavin's, offered a professional suggestion. "David, you must understand that sometimes people do things in the heat of anger, even long-held anger. They justify their positions. They are not evil. They are often drowning in sorrow or an anger that drives them to express it. What your mother saw and experienced in the camps at such an impressionable age would scar her for life. I believe she was attempting to transcend her experience by righting the wrongs. In her mind, and that of the other women, they were doing away with evil. When one is abused and weakened, and suddenly able to transcend the abuse and weakness toward a measure of self-actualization, the effect can be almost hypnotic."

No one responded. She allowed her words to linger for a moment. "There is something else of importance," she said, again reaching into her briefcase to take out the two parcels the various items were delivered in.

"What do you have?" David asked.

"This one you should recognize. It is the parcel you sent to your Uncle Gavin, am I right?" Donna queried. "This *is* your handwriting, is it not?"

David glanced at the parcel. "Yes. This is clearly the one I sent."

Donna nodded. "Then whose handwriting is on this one?" she asked, presenting the parcel sent to Gavin's nieces.

"I don't know," David replied slowly.

Corrine bent forward to get a better look. "That looks like Aunt Helen's handwriting," she finally offered.

David turned to his wife in surprise. "Are you sure?"

"I'm certain. I've seen her handwriting numerous times."

"How would she have come into possession of the birth certificates, a marriage certificate, and the other items in the second parcel?" Donna asked.

"I wouldn't know. We will surely have to ask her," David said with a puzzled look. He noted the time on his watch before turning to Corrine. "Where do you think she would be right now?"

"Where she is every Saturday morning. At the cemetery laying out flowers."

"Yes, of course. I almost forgot. I think we need to walk over there and find her."

Corrine explained. "Aunt Helen has taken over my mother-in-law's duty of placing a flower at each marker in the cemetery every Saturday morning."

"I see," said Donna. "So you think we will find her there now?"

"We should," said David. "It's only a short walk through the woods. There's a path to the cemetery we can take. She should still be there."

The four left the cabin, with Donna and Gavin following David and Corrine on a well-worn path through a wooded area before coming to a wrought iron enclosure, beautifully scrolled toward the top. It was the cemetery. David entered a gate, one of three on the property. While David looked for Aunt Helen, Donna wandered the cemetery's length toward the main entrance. It was a beautifully manicured property, with markers bearing the names of the dead, most with a flower in a simple holder, an indication of Aunt Helen's presence. When approaching the main entrance, Donna noted a plaque on the inside wall, a dedication plaque reading: *These memorial gardens serve to honor the memory of Sarah Mariah Sonntag in her service to the few, affecting the many. April 3rd, 1906 – November 26th, 1946.*

Donna noticed another dedication plaque while she ambled through the gardens, this one dedicated to Ilse Kruin Kaiser, September 3rd, 1887 – June 24th, 1949. Donna noted the last name was the same as the community. On a hunch, she made a call to a trusted and competent advisor, and was assured the information she sought would be quickly forthcoming. Ending the call, she observed David and Corrine walking toward her with Aunt Helen and Gavin.

"We found her," David announced. "She was just finishing up, but wants to rest. Let's head to the benches over there," he said, pointing to an especially appealing corner of the garden.

When they had settled in, Aunt Helen looked at Donna. "It's nice to see you and Gavin again. I wasn't told you were coming to visit. I understand you have questions."

Donna looked at the woman who was such a strong influence in David's life. She was a beauty, even in her aging years. There was a strong determination in her countenance. Her body language communicated strength, fortitude, and resilience. There was still a story to tell, and Aunt Helen was the storyteller, Donna had no doubt.

"You look well," Donna proceeded, treading carefully to start.

"I feel well," Aunt Helen responded. "My dizziness has been addressed successfully. It turned out to be an inner ear infection."

Donna looked about her, at Gavin's, David's, and Corrine's expressions. All looked wary.

"This is a beautiful memorial setting, a loving expression of remembrance," Donna continued, grasping for words.

"Thank you," Aunt Helen replied without further explanation.

"The layout is striking," Donna complemented. "It was configured as the Star of David."

"Impressive. Not many people notice that fact," was Aunt Helen's reply.

Donna noted David cocking his head. "I certainly never noticed it myself, and I've been here countless times."

"I also noticed the memorial plaque to Sarah Sonntag just inside the gates of the garden. Can you tell us who she was? How this garden eventually came to bear her name?"

Aunt Helen looked at Donna intently, conjuring up a reply. Eventually, she simply sighed. "I see it is time to tell the story."

"There is one, isn't there?" Donna replied softly. "You wrote the letter to Carl's daughters, didn't you?"

"Yes, at Ida's request. It is a story that should be told. In fact, your mother, David, wanted it to be revealed after her passing."

"That was the reason for the first parcel, then?" Corrine asked.

Aunt Helen took a deep breath. "Correct. Before leaving the camps, a group of women prisoners, twenty in all, including your mother, David, made a pact to address the unspeakable behavior of the camp overseers. They started with the most egregious violators. Within four years all on their list were tracked down and killed."

"My God!" David said.

"The one list titled *Kapos* were the forty who were done away with by the twenty prisoners, and the other list of numbers were those of the women who made the resolve. The numbers were those stamped on their arms by the SS when they entered the camps. Am I correct?" Donna asked.

"Precisely. The group referred to themselves as the sisters, with your mother taking the lead, a role she fulfilled competently for the rest of her days. Sarah Sonntag uncovered the plot of the sisters, but never revealed it to her dying day, except to her brother Rudolf and sister Frieda.

David stood up aghast. "Oh my God! I get it now! These sisters were our neighbors! For as long as I can remember, they were part of our community. Many were very good to me and my sister. I can't believe they were assassins!"

Aunt Helen smiled kindly at David. She could see his struggle to comprehend the unthinkable. David, sweet David. Protected against all evil by the fierce devotion of his mother, who understood, only too well, the machinations of those in power with sick minds.

"They were sisters of the scorned, David! How easy it is for one to utter a statement of shock, even disgust, when cocooned in protection all your life. How does one who has not known a day of want even begin to comprehend the insult, the deprivation, and the desolation of attempted genocide?"

The words stung, softening David's stance. "Surely the war crime trials addressed the guilty ones," David argued, his voice more subdued.

"Did they? How much do you know about the war crime trials, David?" Aunt Helen asked, already knowing the answer.

David remained quiet. "There was Nuremberg," he said finally.

"Yes. The site of the International Military Tribunal. The trials lasted one year, from October 1945 to October 1946. Twenty-two major Nazi figures were tried, of which twelve were sentenced to death, seven were sentenced to prison, and three were acquitted.

"Now, think about this David. Six million Jews were exterminated, but only twenty-two Nazis were brought to justice at Nuremberg."

"There had to be more trials than Nuremberg," David declared.

"Numerous trials, in fact," Aunt Helen agreed, nodding. "There were twelve war crime trials held at Nuremberg following the International Military Tribunal, lasting two and a half years. This time 177 defendants were tried, but with only ninety-seven convictions. The British also tried the staff of the Bergen-Belsen concentration camp. While there were forty-five defendants, only eleven were sentenced to death by hanging and fourteen were acquitted. The list goes on. There were many efforts to address the atrocities, even by the German government. To date, Germany has tried over 90,000 defendants and served penalty on over 64,000."

"There you have it, then," David railed. "Justice was served. These *sisters*, as you refer to them, had no right to act on their own."

"The difference is, David, the targets of the twenty women, the *sisters*, were prisoners themselves, who acted in an unspeakable manner toward their fellow captives," Donna interjected.

Aunt Helen looked at Donna. "You have studied this, then?"

"I have," Donna answered. "The kapos were as hated as the SS."

"More so. For your mother and the other women, the kapos they targeted were felonious on all levels. They had to pay with their lives."

CHAPTER TWENTY-EIGHT

"Without memory, there is no culture. Without
memory, there would be no civilization, no
society, no future."

Elie Wiesel

It was near noon. Aunt Helen suggested lunch and offered
sandwiches at her home. Gavin was glad for the break. His head
was hurting from the onslaught of heavily loaded information.
David wasn't faring much better. He was quiet and sullen throughout
lunch. Corrine and Aunt Helen talked as though nothing had
transpired, although the women would glance occasionally in
David's direction. Donna was watching on the sidelines, offering a
comment or two when asked about lunch choices.

Donna had still not shared her most disturbing discovery, even
to Gavin, but knew before the end of day, it too would produce
reverberation. Just before the sandwiches were placed on the table,
her cell phone rang. She noted the number and took the call outside
away from listening ears. It was revealing, to say the least.

After lunch dishes were cleared, Donna determined the course
of the afternoon. When offered dessert by Aunt Helen who was
hovering over the kitchen table, she politely declined. "No thank
you, Heide."

Aunt Helen froze in place. All movement between the two women had stopped. Donna continued to hold Aunt Helen's galvanizing gaze.

Corrine noted the exchange. "Oh, Donna, your mind must be elsewhere. This is Aunt Helen, not Heide."

Donna returned Aunt Helen's penetrating glare. "Is Corrine correct, Heide? Would you care to offer a comment? Now would be the time, Heide."

At this, David became alert. "What's going on here? Donna, you know perfectly well this is Aunt Helen. Who is this Heide?"

The silence between the two women was finally broken. "Heide, will you explain to your nephew, or shall I?" Donna said before long.

Aunt Helen dropped her head in a gesture of surrender and sat down. "It was only a matter of time," she uttered under her breath, but audible enough for the others to hear.

"Someone needs to explain," Gavin announced, annoyingly.

Donna looked at Aunt Helen. The struggle for the aging woman was apparent, a woman hiding her true identity all these years. Her gaze was fixed, struggling against admission, as though a veil covered her eyes and countenance.

Donna then made a startling statement. "David, Corrine, and Gavin—meet Heide Goebbels, the youngest daughter of Joseph Goebbels, Reich Minister of Propaganda for Nazi Germany from 1933 to 1945."

The group did not fully understand the announcement. They struggled to comprehend Donna's declaration. Slowly the words took hold, but very slowly. David shook his head, trying to recall history from over seventy years ago. Gavin was just a step or two ahead of him, but remained quiet, his eyes fixed on Aunt Helen.

"You will have to explain this, Donna. I don't think I can take anymore," David said with more than a hint of agitation.

"I'm not following you Donna, but I think we should be insulted," Corrine added.

Donna understood everyone was blindsided. She began to slowly explain. "Joseph Goebbels was the most loyal of Hitler's henchmen. He and his wife Magda, another loyalist, had six children, five daughters and a son. Though their marriage was often tempestuous, they produced Helga, the oldest daughter, Hildegard, Helmut, a son, Holde, Hedda, and Heide, the youngest. There was another son, Harald Quandt, from Magda's previous marriage. In fact Harald, at ten years old, acted as best man at his mother's wedding to Joseph Goebbels. He later served as a lieutenant in the Luftwaffe. He was one of two children of the Goebbels who would survived the Second World War. The rest, along with their parents, perished."

"How? How did they perish?" Corrine asked softly, still struggling with the barrage of information. Her moist eyes, as well as the others, were riveted on Aunt Helen who remained absolutely still.

Donna offered no comment, although she knew the outcome. She waited for Aunt Helen to offer an explanation, to unveil a secret kept for years. Before long, Aunt Helen lifted her head and stared beyond, finally offering a summary. Donna noted the dignified woman had suddenly aged, her regal face taking on a gray cast. For years she'd anticipated this moment. It was finally here.

"They were put to death by my parents the day after Hitler and Eva Braun committed suicide. It was accomplished with a morphine injection at first, to knock them out. A cyanide capsule was placed in their mouths as they slept."

There was stunned silence from the listeners at first. "How horrible! What became of your parents?" Corrine inquired, her voice shaky with emotion.

"They committed suicide in the gardens outside the bunker after confirming the children were dead. My father shot himself. My mother bit down on a cyanide capsule."

The group was immobilized momentarily by the ghastly revelation. After a time David asked, "How did you manage to survive?"

It was obvious Aunt Helen couldn't go on. "May I?" Donna inquired gently of the aging woman. Aunt Helen nodded weakly, wringing her hands and dabbing her eyes with a tissue.

Donna continued the summary. "The entire Goebbels family, six days before their deaths, moved into living quarters on the other end of Hitler's bunker. For the Goebbels, nothing less than unconditional devotion and obedience to the dictates and premise of the Nazi party and its leader was acceptable. To be taken by the Soviet army was unthinkable. Their resolve to go down with the Führer was well known, especially to the inner circle.

"Many people tried to talk Magda out of her decision to put the children to death. Albert Speer, Minister of Armaments and War Production, visited Magda the day before it happened with an offer to squire her and the children away to a safe place. She refused. An appeal by one of Hitler's secretaries, as well as Eva Braun's maid, to entrust the children to their care was flatly rejected."

"Someone had to have intervened if you survived, Aunt Helen," David commented. "Do you know who?"

With effort, Aunt Helen answered, "It was a clandestine effort on the part of our nanny, and the doctor charged with administering the lethal injection of morphine and cyanide."

"Do you know the particulars?" Donna asked, hoping Aunt Helen was willing to be forthcoming. "Has anyone shared the details with you? I was able to find a light reference or two to the rumored survival of one of the children, but no real confirmation."

"I can give you the details," Aunt Helen answered, speaking with more strength. "My nanny, Frieda Brier, convinced the doctor to give me a light injection of morphine, enough to put me to sleep for a time. It was the doctor who made confirmation to my parents that all six of us children were dead. My parents, upon inspection, were convinced we were all dead. Not having followed orders to the letter would have meant the doctor's death, but he took the chance. When my parents took their lives the next day, Frieda quickly substituted my body for that of a dead female child near to my age found in the bombing, substituting her clothes for my white dress.

"Frieda Brier has a marker in the cemetery," David noted.

"Frieda Brier was the sister of Sarah Sonntag, David. It was Sonntag who arranged for me to be cared for and raised by your mother and the sisters. Her brother, Rudolf, squired me away from Berlin for safety."

"Is that why the cemetery is so named?"

"Yes," came the reply. Aunt Helen then turned to Donna. "What made you suspicious?"

Donna sat back, giving the question thought. She wanted to be kind to this woman. There was no reason not to be. She had been in hiding for a lifetime because of circumstances beyond her control, including the madness of her parents.

"Two things, really. First, the handwriting on the second parcel matched the handwriting on the letter included in the first, but not on the parcel itself. It was your handwriting."

"The second thing?" Gavin asked.

"Remember our July 4th barbecue this past year, when Aunt Helen fell ill? We took her to the guest room to rest. She insisted on resting on top of the bedspread, so I provided a light covering. If you remember, periodically I checked in on her while she slept. At one point, the covers slipped from her feet. When I went to adjust them, I noticed a tattoo on the plantar surface of her big toe."

"How odd. What was it?" David inquired, looking at Aunt Helen all the while.

"The symbol of the Nazi party, the swastika."

"Who would do such a thing?" David asked, repelled by the answer.

Aunt Helen looked at her nephew. "My mother. All of us children had the tattoo applied upon birth."

"Who in a million years would tattoo their children with a symbol of atrocity?" Corrine questioned.

Aunt Helen provided the answer. Her manner was subdued, her voice quietly commanding. "To those who suffered under Hitler, it became a symbol of atrocity, that is true However, the Germans were not the first to make use of the design. It has, in fact, a 12,000-year history as a good luck symbol in almost every culture in the world.

"For Hitler it represented renewal for the Germanic Aryan race. He was resolute in his belief the Jews had undermined the Aryan heritage of Germany, taking away its rightful place in history. He was determined to correct what he believed to be a miscarriage of justice."

Aunt Helen sighed deeply before speaking again, an effort, in Donna's mind, to assemble her thoughts and strength. When she spoke, her voice was constant and strong. "You can trust I have done extensive reading of the time period, and especially that of my parents. My father, Joseph Goebbels, is considered to have been the most loyal of Hitler's inner circle. The others abandoning him, even making deals for their freedom toward the end. My father's diaries give insight as to his thinking and the unfolding of the war. A chilling read, if I might add. My mother, on the other hand, appeared to be a lost soul of sorts, clinging to a devotion to Hitler bearing no sensibility."

"I agree," Donna interjected softly, mindful of the conversation's emotional tone. "Magda Goebbels was the only wife among Nazi leadership to end, not only her life, but that of five of her six children, in a final salute to the Nazi ideology. As a psychiatrist, I remain intrigued by her motivation. I can only guess she was unable to identify with herself. She, in my opinion, filtered her thoughts and actions through the eyes of others. On the other hand, she had an attraction to power and charisma. It explains her alliance with her husband, Joseph Goebbels, and the worshipful relationship she had with Hitler."

Aunt Helen hung her head, deep in thought before she spoke again. "I have gone over the final days of the Nazi regime over and over again. I have read everything written on my parents. How many times I have reviewed the steps of my survival, as told to me by your mother, David. I came to learn about a nanny and doctor who feigned my death, as well as an intermediary, Sarah Sonntag, who found a surrogate family, Ida Tandermann and the sisters, who faithfully cared for me for many years."

"When did she tell you of your true identity?" David asked.

"I will answer your question and many more, but first I have a need to rest. I'm afraid the conversations has exhausted me."

Corrine escorted Aunt Helen to her bedroom and returned to the kitchen. "I feel as though I've entered the twilight zone," Corrine commented as she took a seat again at the table.

David and Gavin didn't respond. Gavin and Donna were watching David, who seemed to be a million miles away. "My mother and my so-called 'aunts' were vigilantes. My favorite aunt is the only living survivor of a high-ranking Nazi war criminal. It seems I have to rethink my entire childhood!"

Donna observed how disturbed David was.

"Not necessarily," Gavin returned before she could respond. "Although parts of it may have to be reframed in light of this new information."

"Starting with my mother and the sisters!"

David was so unsettled, he announced to Donna, Gavin, and Corrine that he was going for a walk while Aunt Helen rested. He didn't suggest company and they didn't offer. They understood his need to process. David found himself at the cemetery. Seeing it, as if for the first time, he began to walk its parameters, looking at each marker, remembering his youth. There were so many "aunts" he recalled with fondness, women who were good to him and his sister. He remembered the parties at the community center, the celebrations, the dances, and the weddings, as well as the funerals, the illnesses, and accidents occasioning community support. He remembered faces, and shared experiences of triumph and loss, of celebration and tears, of heartbreak and renewal. He remembered and he cried, finding a seat on a bench nearby to unload his bewilderment. How was it he was never told of his mother's real past or that of the aunts? Did his father know? The questions poured into his mind only to release more tears.

David felt disconnected, discounted, and even betrayed by a history kept from him. "Would it have made a difference if I had known earlier?" he asked himself. After a time, he had an insight, an awakening, and awareness of his mother's need to protect him from knowledge better saved for a later time. The realization brought comfort. He went to his parents' grave and knelt in prayer, something he hadn't done in a very long time. He then moved on to other markers in the cemetery, to those connected to the greatest memories and joy. The effort calmed him. He drew in a long breath, abandoning the confines of doubt to reclaim and recollect himself before returning to Aunt Helen's home.

CHAPTER TWENTY-NINE

"I decided to devote my life to telling the
story because I felt that having survived I owe
something to the dead. Anyone who does not
remember betrays them again."

Elie Wiesel

Upon David's return to Aunt Helen's home, he found the others at the kitchen table with a plate of cookies and cups of coffee in front of them. Aunt Helen, looking more rested, eyed her nephew with concern, mindful of the effect the day's revelations may have had on him. She was relieved when he approached her with a kiss on the cheek.

"I failed to thank you for the delicious lunch," was all he said before joining the others at the table. Gavin, having taken a bite of his cookie, nodded approvingly at this nephew.

Donna had something on her mind, a conclusion she reached early on when she suspected who Aunt Helen really was. This seemed like the perfect opportunity to broach the subject. "I think we all need to consider the grave ramifications that could result if it became public knowledge that Aunt Helen is really the youngest daughter of Magda and Joseph Goebbels," she said without preamble.

The look of relief spreading across Aunt Helen's face was obvious. Discovery was her greatest fear.

"What do you mean?" Corrine asked. "What grave results?"

Gavin sat back, pondering the situation. "Donna is right," was all he said.

"I don't understand. What am I missing?" Corrine returned.

Donna waited for a response from the others, before finally answering. "I am responsible for uncovering this bombshell. I understood immediately, however, that revealing it could place Aunt Helen in danger from those who still harbor hatred and animosity toward the Nazi regime."

"Do you mean she could be assassinated?" Corrine queried with a sound of alarm.

"Most definitely," Gavin returned.

David, too, had been thoughtful. "At the very least, she wouldn't have a minute's peace, and neither would our community. News agencies from around the world would camp outside our homes for the chance of a glimpse or an interview with the daughter of one of the world's most notorious promotors of German propaganda during Hitler's rule. It would amount to nothing less than madness for all of us."

"That being said," Donna continued with a note of authority, "I propose we confine this information to a small circle of us."

"Yes, I agree," Corrine said.

The four assured Aunt Helen of their support of her continued anonymity. Aunt Helen dabbed away her tears, grateful for their loyalty.

"There are things you should know, David. Things your mother wanted revealed after her passing," Aunt Helen began after collecting herself.

"You mean there is more?" David cried out incredulously.

Aunt Helen stood. "Follow me," she beckoned the group.

They were escorted into Aunt Helen's bedroom. She stood in front of the stone fireplace, one of two in the home. The other was in the living room. She looked at David. "You lived in this home until your marriage to Corrine. In all of that time, and since, have you ever seen a fire in this fireplace?" she asked her nephew.

"I don't recall that I ever did," he answered perplexed.

"There's a reason you never did." With a light gesture, Aunt Helen removed a small stone on the fireplace to reveal a button and a small crank. When she pressed the button, the entire front of the fireplace began to move to the side to reveal a well-established safe of considerable size."

"What in the world?" David asked with disbelief. The others looked at each other questioningly as they peered into the cavity of the fireplace.

Aunt Helen then used the crank to open the safe, an ingenious one-of-a-kind design requiring no electricity. She reached in for a roll of papers secured by a simple elastic band. She then looked at Gavin. "These papers will identify the list of numbers against the list of names sent to you shortly after your sister's death."

Gavin's demeanor suddenly became unsettled. "What will it reveal?"

Donna answered for the woman. "I suspect it will reveal the numbers assigned to your mother and the sisters while in the camps."

Aunt Helen nodded in agreement. "There are other lists, I'm afraid."

"These would be—?" Gavin asked without finishing his sentence.

Aunt Helen turned to Donna to supply the answer. "They will identify the killer of each of the kapos on the list."

"Yes, however, there are not forty names, but forty-one. An additional name was added," Aunt Helen offered.

"Who was it?" Corrine asked.

Aunt Helen looked at her nephew and grew a bit hesitant. She then ventured on, not wanting to leave anything out. "That one was not a kapo, but a betrayer. It was a neighbor and one-time friend of Ilse Kaiser. Her name was Dagfried Soffell. Ida had discovered she was the one who had betrayed Ms. Kaiser and her family by telling the SS that your mother and her parents were in hiding in Ms. Kaiser's home. Ida blamed Soffell for the deaths of Ilse's father and sister, and for the deaths of her parents as well. She personally took responsibility for eliminating the woman."

Gavin slumped to a sitting position on the bed, completely unnerved by the explanation. David didn't look much better than his uncle. Everyone had gone quiet.

It was Gavin who finally spoke, looking up at Aunt Helen, whose face remained expressionless. "I thought it odd at the time when David commented on my first visit that my sister had willed lifetime residence of her home to you, despite the fact that you lived just up the road. Now I understand."

"I'm glad *you* do. I still don't get it," David said with a hint of irritation.

Aunt Helen smiled at her nephew, understanding his confusion. "It is simple, really. My home did not have a safe. Your mother felt it was the prudent course to protect her history and that of the sisters by having me live here until my death. Then the contents of the safe would remain secure until that time, after which all could be revealed."

"I asked this question earlier," Donna ventured forth, "but I am still curious. When did you come to learn of your history and that of the others?"

"Believe it or not, I was forty-five years old, a day I will never forget. Your mother arranged a birthday party for me. It took place in the Community Center and was attended by women only."

"My mother and the sisters," David concluded quickly.

"Precisely. The party had a purpose. It would be the day I would find out who I really was, my history and that of my parents, and why they needed to protect me."

"I can't imagine the effect such a revelation would have on you," Donna replied.

"It was a bombshell, I can assure you, but then each of my 'aunts' shared what I meant to her and how I had given each a purpose in life. It was a moving experience. I realized, even though my past was tainted with notoriety because of my parents' devotion to Hitler, I was singled out and surrounded by caring ones, by those Hitler had targeted. I received the best education, for example, earning a master's in both accounting and economics."

"Did you ever marry?" Gavin asked.

"Briefly. My husband was killed in Vietnam a year after we married."

"I remember him," David said softly, "as being very kind." He looked at his aunt as if for the first time.

Aunt Helen returned to the safe. She gingerly reached in to retrieve a small, ornately carved wooden box. She placed it on the bed and asked everyone to gather around. Carefully unlocking the box she opened it to reveal what appeared to be a medal. She took the item and placed it on a red, velvet cloth she kept with it.

"What is it?" David asked. "It looks like a medal."

"It is."

"It's beautiful, very military, and with the swastika in the middle." Corrine observed.

They passed around a beautifully detailed gold medal for each to have a close look before looking to Aunt Helen for an explanation.

When it was returned to her by Gavin, she held it reverently in her hand, looking at it with an odd expression on her face. After a hesitating moment, she offered an explanation.

"On the morning of April 30th, 1945, the day Hitler took his own life, he said a final goodbye to those who faithfully remained. My mother and father were among them. As it was told to me, Hitler shook my mother's hand and, with shaking hands, he took the gold party insignia from his gray army coat and transferred it to the lapel of my mother's jacket, proclaiming her the 'First Mother of the Reich'. Then my mother broke down in tears. The transfer of the gold party insignia was the highest honor ever paid a woman of the Third Reich. Immediately after my parents' suicide, the insignia was taken from my mother's lapel by Sarah Sonntag and Frieda Brier's brother, Rudolf Coble, the personal guard and courier for my father, Joseph Goebbels."

"The insignia was given to your mother, David, for safe-keeping until she felt I was ready to receive it and know its implications. She gave it to me on the day of my forty-fifth birthday celebration."

"My God!" Corrine declared, raising her hands to her face in disbelief. "That's another reason to protect you, Aunt Helen. Collectors would give their right arms for this piece of history!"

"That's assuming Hitler did not replace this with another just before his death," Aunt Helen replied, revealing her knowledge of the subject. "It is assumed he had many such pins, so their value is questionable. It is, however, a piece of history, and more special because it was given to my mother."

Once again, Aunt Helen reached into the safe and struggled to pull out a very heavy strongbox. Gavin helped her transfer the box to the bed, but even for him it was a chore. When she opened it, the group gasped in awe. They were staring at German gold coins. Many of them!

CHAPTER THIRTY

"Friendship marks a life even more deeply than love. Love risks degenerating into obsession, friendship is never anything but sharing."

Elie Wiesel, The Gates of the Forest

David looked at the coins, then at Aunt Helen, and again the coins. "Where did these come from?"

"When your mother shared the contents of this safe with me, two years before she died, that was my question as well. Her answer surprised me, and still sends shivers up my spine," Aunt Helen shared.

"Well?" an impatient David pressed.

"Rudolf Coble stole it from Hitler's bunker," came the reply.

"Coble was the personal bodyguard for your father, Joseph Goebbels," Donna confirmed.

"Yes," Aunt Helen returned, "and instrumental in securing my safety, along with his two sisters, Sarah and Frieda, before I was entrusted to the care of your mother."

"How much is here?" Gavin asked, still staring down at the coins.

"I haven't taken the time to count it, but it is the residual of a still very healthy Swiss bank account set up when a portion of the stolen gold was transferred to your mother, a noble act of Mr. Coble's before your mother came to America."

"Why would he do such a thing? He hardly knew David's mother," Corrine queried.

"The answer will surprise you, but the long and the short of it is that he came, over time, to hate Hitler for the suffering of millions of people. More especially he hated my parents, Magda and Joseph Goebbels, for murdering their children. In his mind, the gold could be put to better use to uplift and restore some of those who suffered.

"You should know he lost his leg to an infection from an injury he incurred as he was escaping Berlin with me when the Russians entered the city. He and Frieda Brier took me all the way to the Netherlands. Frieda, you should know, was my nanny and was instrumental, along with the doctor, in my survival. Having reached the Netherlands, it was agreed after a time that Frieda would take the child back to Berlin. Rudolf's condition, however, was too severe for him to travel. This is how he came to stay with Ms. Kaiser, the woman who gave a home to your mother after her camp experience."

"I see. So Rudolf knew about the sisters' plan?" Donna asked.

"Through Sarah Sonntag, yes. His love for me and my deceased siblings afforded him an outlet for his hatred."

"Who has been managing the Swiss bank account since my mother's death?" David asked, still trying to wrap his head around what seemed to be unceasing staggering revelations.

"Your mother was a shrewd woman, David. I came to understand her leanings and motivation. Her interest in my education, in my obtaining a master's degree in both accounting and economics, was so that I could eventually manage affairs until such time as you could take over."

"Me?" David replied, shocked by the implications. "Corrine can tell you I barely manage to balance my checkbook!"

"You will have my assistance for as long as it takes," Aunt Helen replied. "You should be aware, however, that all of Kaiser Commons, along with the surrounding property purchased over the years, is owned by Tandermann Holdings, which is also the name of the Swiss bank account."

"Do you mean no one person individually owns the homes in the village?" Gavin asked.

"That is correct. Every sister was provided a home once she came here, but never owned it. The taxes, upkeep, and maintenance were paid by Tandermann Holdings for as long as they lived. Their medical and dental care was also provided by Tandermann Holdings for their entire lives after they moved to America."

"All of the sisters are gone now. What has become of the homes? They still look well maintained," Donna questioned.

"They are leased, but never sold. The location of Kaiser Commons and surrounding acreage makes it very desirable to developers, especially because of its proximity to the highway. Your mother had vision. The developers knock on our door often."

"Tandermann Holdings has considerable assets, and is worth millions," Donna reported to David and Gavin.

"You know this, how?" Aunt Helen asked Donna.

"A friend of mine is a forensic financial investigator. On a hunch, I telephoned him yesterday to see what he could find out about Kaiser Commons. His report was revealing, to say the least."

"Your hunches are almost scary, Donna," Gavin said.

"I agree," Aunt Helen said. "It will be of interest to you, Mr. Tandermann, that your sister provided for the children and grandchildren of her two brothers, even though she purposely did not come forward to you and your brother, Carl, because of her past."

"For which I am saddened," Gavin returned. "I'd like to think we would have understood."

BELLA FAYRE

"Your being employed by the FBI made her cautious. At the same time, she was protecting me."

"What became of Mr. Coble?" Donna asked, trying to make sense of it all.

"Rudolf is buried in the cemetery next to his sisters. Which reminds me—," Aunt Helen said, reaching into the safe again to draw out a well-worn journal.

"When your mother made plans to marry your father, Rudolf and Frieda were invited to the wedding and they accepted. Your mother not only wanted their blessing, but also asked Frieda and Rudolf to bring the remains of their deceased sister, Sarah, for burial on the grounds of Sonntag Memorial Garden. This was done."

"From what your mother shared, the ceremonies for both the wedding and the final internment of Sarah's ashes were more than memorable. It was an occasion, however, for Rudolf to reveal his own plan.

"Before your mother left for America, Rudolf gave her a list. It turned out to contain the names of Nazis who fled to America and were now in hiding. He wanted the sisters to deal with it as they had done with the kapos."

"You're kidding?" David blurted in disbelief. "You mean he wanted them to kill those on his list, too?"

"Something like that," Aunt Helen confirmed, "however most of the sisters refused."

"Most? Was my mother among them?"

Aunt Helen nodded. "She was the first to refuse. She had found a new life with Jacob and wanted no reminder of the past. In an acknowledgement of Mr. Coble's numerous gestures of support and goodwill, she urged Rudolf and Frieda to live with them in the village. This they did."

"What about the list?" Corrine asked almost in a whisper.

208

"Mr. Coble found a way to deal with them. It was never talked about and no one asked, but before he died, Rudolf Coble revealed he had overseen a network of operatives, mostly camp survivors, who secretly hunted down those in hiding. Several of the sisters assisted. This," Aunt Helen gestured with the journal in her hand, "are the names of concentration camp guards, for the most part, who were in hiding, all now dead."

"How is this information relevant?" Donna asked, intrigued by the news.

Aunt Helen betrayed a sly smile. "Follow me," she beckoned her listeners.

David's face turned gray. "I don't think I'm going to like this," he said to no one in particular.

Aunt Helen led them to the basement door and then down the steps. She approached the closets lining one of the walls and opened a set of closet doors. Pushing clothing to the side, she stepped back to allow the group to see another door deep within, a steel door.

"Uh oh! This looks ominous," David commented.

Aunt Helen then unlocked the steel door with a key hidden in the closet to reveal a large, round steel cylinder.

"What's all this?" Gavin asked.

Aunt Helen answered after taking in the puzzled looks of her listeners. "It is my understanding that this whole community was built to protect the sisters in the event that the deeds they committed after their camp experience became public. It allows for escape. It is why this home, and the home directly across the street—the first two homes built in this community;— are different from the rest in Kaiser Commons. There is a line of connecting cylinders forming a tunnel that begin here and end in the basement of the Community Center. The home across the street has exactly the same provision. It was where Mr. Coble resided. Neither escape tunnel was ever used, but to Mr. Coble, it provided additional reassurance as he set up his U.S.-based operation to hunt down German war criminals."

David looked stunned. "All this time, I thought we were normal people leading normal, happy lives."

Aunt Helen looked softly at her nephew. "David, despite the history, you and your sister had an idyllic upbringing, surrounded and protected by grownups who loved you. You played with other children whose lives were as perfect as their parents could make them, despite the memories. This," she said, sweeping her hand in the direction of the tunnel, "was simply a precaution. Your mother made sure there was always a back-up plan for the back-up plan."

"So, I assume none of the sisters betrayed the secret," Donna concluded.

"None. They were upstanding people putting the past behind them. They remained supportive of each other until the last of them, your mother, died. I was privileged to be trusted enough to carry the knowledge of their past. I never judged them. I saw them as heroes."

Donna, ever thoughtful, offered a parting comment. "Some do judge, Aunt Helen. There are those who have never experienced the whip across their back, the hunger from deprivation, the illness from a diseased-state brought on by non-existent medical care. They have never experienced the pain of basic human need ripped from them inhumanly, or the sub-human demand for them to act as slaves in unspeakable acts to insure their very survival. This is what the camps offered."

Aunt Helen looked at Donna for a long moment before she responded. "The end result, once one gets beyond the acts of retaliation, is considerable. The sisters are represented in the form of charities, donations, and foundations through Tandermann Holdings. Each one was granted a sub-account in Tandermann Holdings and encouraged to support charitable organizations of their choosing. Regardless of your conclusion as to the actions of the sisters, as a group they formulated an impressive outpouring of support that continues to this day, over one thousand, in fact."

"Much of it due to Hitler's gold, I would think," Gavin responded.

"It was put to good use, Mr. Tandermann. I have been proud to serve its interests and the intent of the sisters of the scorned."

CHAPTER THIRTY-ONE

"It happened to fast. The ghetto. The deportation.
The sealed cattle car. The fiery altar upon which
the history of our people and the future of
mankind were meant to be sacrificed."

Elie Wiesel

Two Years Later

Gavin, Carole, Donna, and Ken found themselves attending the memorial service for Aunt Helen. She had died in her sleep from a massive stroke two weeks earlier and would be buried beside her husband, who gave his life in service to his country in Vietnam over forty years ago.

For Donna, Gavin's phone call of Aunt Helen's passing brought about a profound sadness. Occasions to reflect on the events of Aunt Helen, Ida Tandermann, and the sisters conjured up conflicting emotion, but it always brought her back to the eventual strength of humanity.

As she and Ken stood on a misty spring morning in Sonntag Memorial Garden with Aunt Helen's loved ones, Donna would recall the telling of the sisters by the real Aunt Helen, Heide Goebbels. Walking the cemetery after the service, she recognized names on markers from Aunt Helen's and David's recounting of memory: Rudolf Coble, Frieda Brier, Sarah Sonntag, Ilse Kaiser, and Jacob Schmidt. There were others.

A year before Aunt Helen's passing, she honored her supporters by placing a plaque decorously in the cemetery. It bore, in regal presentation, the names of each of the sisters. Alongside each name was an etched number; their number tattooed while in the camps. To Aunt Helen, the number remained their strength and fortitude. It was her determination the numbers would ultimately serve as a tribute to the sisters, once scorned, but ultimately freed on so many levels in the human experience.

Months before her death Aunt Helen would present to David another packet, this time a personal, handwritten recounting of each of the sisters' camp experiences. The readings, intense and soulful, would drive him to his knees in tears, especially those of his mother.

Over time, he would understand their suffering and degradation, as well as their motivation. He would reflect on the glory of his childhood, one uninterrupted by the pains of diabolical forces, and give thanks to the benevolent rendering of a mother who transcended the once-scorned.

Elie Wiesel's Nobel Peace Prize Acceptance Speech
Oslo, Norway – December 10, 1986

It is with a profound sense of humility that I accept the honor you have chosen to bestow upon me. I know: your choice transcends me. This both frightens and pleases me.

It frightens me because I wonder: do I have the right to represent the multitudes who have perished? Do I have the right to accept this great honor on their behalf? ... I do not. That would be presumptuous. No one may speak for the dead, no one may interpret their mutilated dreams and visions.

It pleases me because I may say that this honor belongs to all the survivors and their children, and through us, to the Jewish people with whose destiny I have always identified.

I remember: it happened yesterday or eternities ago. A young Jewish boy discovered the kingdom of night. I remember his bewilderment, I remember his anguish. It all happened so fast. The ghetto. The deportation. The sealed cattle car. The fiery altar upon which the history of our people and the future of mankind were meant to be sacrificed.

I remember: he asked his father: "Can this be true?" This is the twentieth century, not the Middle Ages. Who would allow such crimes to be committed? How could the world remain silent?

And now the boy is turning to me: "Tell me," he asks. "What have you done with my future? What have you done with your life?"

And I tell him that I have tried. That I have tried to keep memory alive, that I have tried to fight those who would forget. Because if we forget, we are guilty, we are accomplices.

And then I explained to him how naive we were, that the world did know and remain silent. And that is why I swore never to be silent whenever and wherever human beings endure suffering and humiliation. We must always take sides. Neutrality helps the oppressor, never the victim. Silence encourages the tormentor, never the tormented. Sometimes we must interfere. When human lives are endangered, when human dignity is in jeopardy, national borders and sensitivities become irrelevant. Wherever men or women are persecuted because of their race, religion, or political views, that place must—at that moment— become the center of the universe.

Of course, since I am a Jew profoundly rooted in my peoples' memory and tradition, my first response is to Jewish fears, Jewish needs, Jewish crises. For I belong to a traumatized generation, one that experienced the abandonment and solitude of our people. It would be unnatural for me not to make Jewish priorities my own: Israel, Soviet Jewry, Jews in Arab lands ... But there are others as important to me. Apartheid is, in my view, as abhorrent as anti-Semitism. To me, Andrei Sakharov's isolation is as much of a disgrace as Josef Biegun's imprisonment. As is the denial of Solidarity and its leader Lech Walesa's right to dissent. And Nelson Mandela's interminable imprisonment.

"FOR THE DEAD
AND THE LIVING
WE MUST BEAR
WITNESS."

Elie Wiesel

COMMENTS BY
Bella Fayre

My fascination with the time period presented in *Sisters of the Scorned*, is much in part due to my upbringing as the child of German Jewish heritage. Early in my youth, and born after World War II, I would learn my father was the child of a German girl and a Jewish boy who were discouraged from marriage due to discordance in religious upbringing.

Instead, the father of the Jewish boy, as the story was told, gave to the father of the German girl gold coins to assist in the upbringing of the child. The child's grandfather invested the gold coins in German war bonds, a decision which would ultimately prove without gain.

Mindful of the growing political threat toward Jews, my great-grandfather understood a German boy with Jewish blood would not be safe in the current political environment. The boy, now fifteen years old, was placed on a ship bound for America entering his new home in April of 1931.

My father would become a U.S. citizen, eventually marry a woman of German descent, and produce nine children.

SUGGESTED READINGS

Sisters of the Scorned is a work of fiction. The following resources were helpful in understanding the time period, allowing a nuance of political and social leanings though on occasion I took literary license. I recommend the following sources of material, for those interested:

Wiesel, Elie. *Night*. Translated from French by Marion Wiesel, 2006.

Helm, Sarah. *Ravenbrück – Life and Death in Hitler's Concentration Camp for Women,* 2016.

Saidel, Rochelle G. *The Jewish Women of Ravensbrück Concentration Camp*, 2004.

Tusa, Anna and John Tusa. *The Nuremberg Trial*, 1984.

Martin, Roy A. *Inside Nürnberg—Military Justice for Nazi War Crimes,* 2000.

Drucker, Olga Levy. *Kindertransport,* 1992.

Sigmund, Anna Maria. *Women of the Third Reich*, 2000.

Finals Entries 1945 – The Diaries of Joseph Goebbels - 1978

Klabunde, Anja. *Magda Goebbels*, 2001/2003/1999.

Lindwer, Willy. *The Last Seven Months of Anne Frank*, 1988.

Boom, Corrie Ten. *The Hiding Place*, 1977.

IN GRATEFUL ACKNOWLEDGEMENT

I wish to express my deepest appreciation to those who supported me in my writing of *Sisters of the Scorned*.

- My family and friends who never cease to encourage me forward.
- The Carolina Forest Author's Club of Myrtle Beach, South Carolina, who offered their kind suggestions and comments.
- Kathy Dunker, for her suggestions, observations, and overview.
- Michlean Lowy Amir, U.S. Holocaust Memorial Museum Reference Coordinator for pointing me in the right direction.
- Elizabeth VanZwoll for proofreading and editing skills.
- Jessica Wright Tilles for interior layout and book cover design.

Made in the
USA
Columbia, SC

81949994R00138